THE MYSTERY
OF THE
MISSING MASK

M. A. Wilson

Illustrations by Vadym Prokhorenko

Rainy Bay Press
Gibsons, BC

Published by Rainy Bay Press
PO Box 1911
Gibsons, BC
V0N 1V0

www.rainybaypress.ca

ISBN: 978-0-9953445-2-5

To Meg

Table of Contents

~1~

The Grizzly Mask

Claire, Ryan, Kendra, and Nathan watched as Aunt Jennie approached the podium at the front of the room. She took the microphone from the stand and paused a moment as a hush fell over the crowd. The museum was packed with people and some of them had to stand outside, peering through the open doors. A large smile broke out across Aunt Jennie's face as she surveyed the crowd.

"Welcome everyone, to the opening of the new Phillips wing of the Maple Harbour Museum," she began. "It's been a long time coming."

Nathan nudged his sister Claire, who glanced at him with a grin. Their mom had worked for years on the new museum wing. It was one of the reasons she had run for village council. Ever since old Captain Phillips had died and left his collection of valuable maritime antiques to the museum, she had been working to build an extension to the museum where they could be displayed. For many years they had been stored in a warehouse in the city, but today the entire collection would finally be on display in Maple Harbour.

Aunt Jennie kept her speech short, thanking the community for their support in raising the funds to build the new wing. Then she turned over the microphone to the museum curator and stepped to the side. She stood next to a tall, elegant woman. The woman's hair was streaked with grey and she was wearing a colourful shawl draped over her shoulders.

Claire recognized her as Sylvia Francis. She was the daughter of old Captain Phillips and had worked closely with Aunt Jennie in fundraising for the new museum. As the curator began to speak, Sylvia took Aunt Jennie's hand and gave it a squeeze. With her other hand she held on tightly to a boy at her side. He was about the same age as Claire, with short dark hair and wearing jeans and sneakers.

Claire turned her attention back to the curator, who was telling the history of the artifacts. His name was Jim Jenson and he had worked at the museum as long as Claire could remember. He was a tall, thin man with dark curly hair who usually seemed to have a worried look on his face. Now, though, he spoke excitedly about the new collection.

"Of course," the curator said, "the most important item in the collection is the Galiano Grizzly

Mask. This incredibly rare mask is over 200 years old and was collected by the Spanish explorer Dionisio Galiano on his expedition to Nootka Sound in 1792. Later that year he gave it to Captain George Vancouver when they explored Georgia Strait together. Not only is it one of the oldest remaining examples of a coastal First Nations mask, but it is also an important part of our maritime history.

"The mask disappeared shortly after George Vancouver's death. Everyone assumed it was lost forever until Captain Phillips discovered it in a London pawn shop 30 years ago." He paused for a moment.

"Today," he went on, "thanks to the generous bequest of Captain Phillips and the hard work of his daughter, Sylvia Francis, this mask and all of Captain Phillips's collection will be available for everyone to see, right here at the Maple Harbour Museum."

Next to the curator there was a display board which showed a picture of the mask, as well as other items from the collection. The mask had the face of a grizzly bear with its jaws open in a ferocious manner. Even at a distance it looked quite scary, thought Claire.

Jim Jenson finished his speech and invited a tall man in a dark business suit to the podium, introducing him as a representative of the federal government. The man placed a stack of papers in front of him and began to speak. He thanked all those involved and then proceeded to give a long explanation of the importance of the artifacts and what his government had done to make the new museum wing happen.

Nothing about the efforts of everybody here, Claire thought to herself wryly. She thought she could see her mother rolling her eyes, although it might have been her imagination. The man continued to drone on, and after a while the crowd grew restless. Next to her, Nathan began to fidget. Claire gave him an elbow and glared at him.

"I've got to go to the bathroom!" he said under his breath.

"Then go!" she whispered back. "He'll probably still be talking when you get back."

Nathan slipped between the people behind him and made his way to the back of the hall. He looked for the washrooms but couldn't see them. There was a door on one side that looked like it led to a corridor. Nathan pushed his way through the crowd. He opened the door and stepped through, closing the door behind him. At the end of the corridor was a sign indicating washrooms to the right. When he reached the sign he saw another set of doors.

These must lead to the new museum wing, thought Nathan. I wonder if I'm supposed to be in here.

But he couldn't see a washroom, so he pushed the doors open and walked into a darkened hallway. The lights were off, but he could still see by the light coming through windows at the end. Walking slowly, he wondered which of the various doors was the washroom. This part of the building was so new that signs hadn't been put up on the doors yet. Finally, he picked a door at random and pushed it open.

As he stepped forward there was a crash. Opening the door had knocked over a stool with a toolbox on it, and the floor was now covered in tools and electrical parts. On the other side of the room stood a ladder, leading to an opening in the ceiling.

Nathan looked in dismay at the tools lying scattered all over the floor. He knelt down and started to pick them up but stopped as he realized he had no idea where each one was supposed to go. Suddenly he heard a noise from the ceiling. Nathan saw black sneakers with paint splatters on the toes emerge from the opening. He panicked. The owner of those shoes wouldn't be happy when they saw their tools spilled everywhere!

Nathan quickly backed out of the room. Hurrying down the corridor, he pushed open the next door he came to and went in. Luckily, this was the washroom he had been looking for. Locking himself in a stall, he waited anxiously. But there was no sound from the corridor. Eventually, Nathan got up the nerve to poke his head out into the hallway and look around. Seeing nobody, he scurried back to the main hall.

The man from the government was still talking. Nathan worked his way through the crowd and slipped in between Claire and his cousin Ryan.

"You didn't miss much," whispered Ryan with a grin. Much of the audience was no longer paying attention to the speaker and a few people appeared to be dozing off. Nathan didn't say anything about the incident with the toolbox. He was afraid Claire might make him go back and apologize. When the speaker finally finished, the curator stepped up to the podium again.

"And now it's time to open our new museum," he said. "I'd like to call on the members of Captain Phillips's family, his daughter Sylvia and great-grandson Tyler, to come up." Sylvia Francis and the boy at her side stepped forward. Together they held out an oversized pair of scissors and cut a large yellow ribbon that stretched across the museum entrance.

"The museum is officially open!" declared the curator. "Everybody is welcome to go in!" There was a surge of people toward the new wing and soon the main hall was nearly empty. Claire, Ryan, Kendra, and Nathan were carried along with the crowd and soon found themselves inside the museum. There were displays of old telescopes, sextants, compasses, ships' bells, and other maritime artifacts. There was even a case holding Captain Vancouver's favourite pipe, still filled with tobacco. Mounted on the walls were old charts showing the journeys of early explorers up and down the coast of British Columbia.

In the middle of the collection was a glass case with a large crowd gathered around it. Inside it was the Galiano Grizzly Mask. The mask was elaborately carved from a single piece of cedar. Sharp teeth carved from bone jutted out menacingly around a bright red tongue. The mask was inlaid with small pieces of shell and bone surrounding its eyes, which were black with dark red circles in their centres. Up close it seemed even more ferocious and terrifying than it had in the picture.

The children would have liked to have stayed longer, but Aunt Jennie had warned them she had to leave soon for another appointment, so they made their way back to the main hall. She saw them come out and walked over to them.

"Well, what did you think?" she asked.

"Amazing!" said Kendra. "The mask is so realistic and scary."

"And its history is so interesting," said Ryan. "At least the curator's version," he added with a grin.

Aunt Jennie laughed. "That fellow from the government wasn't the most inspiring speaker," she admitted. "But he did do a lot to get the new wing built."

Outside, the sun was shining and the sky was blue with only a few clouds. It had been raining earlier and now the air smelled fresh and clean. They made their way across the parking lot and climbed into Aunt Jennie's car. She started the engine and soon they were driving along the winding road to Rainy Bay.

As they drove, they discussed what they would do for the next few weeks. Ryan and Kendra had just arrived that morning to spend their summer holidays in Maple Harbour with their cousins Claire and Nathan. Life in Maple Harbour was very different from their home in the city, where everything seemed so busy. Here there was plenty of time for mo. important things—like swimming and playing on the beach.

Kendra thought back to all the exciting things that happened to them last year. The previous summer in Maple Harbour they had learned to sail, discovered a sunken wreck, and stopped a gang of art thieves while camping on Whalebone Island. I wonder what kind of adventures we'll get up to this year, she thought.

rprise in the Water

Uncle William was waiting for them outside when they got home. He had been unable to attend the ceremony as he had been out of town for a few days and had just returned. Beside him was Claire and Nathan's dog, Meg, wagging her tail.

Meg was an overly-friendly golden lab who never liked to be left behind. She was a rescue dog from the SPCA and would spend her whole day being petted if given the chance. As soon as the car came to a stop, she rushed over to greet them.

"Meg!" cried Ryan and Kendra together, bending over to give the dog a big hug. Meg pushed up against them, delighted to see them again after all this time.

"Hey, what about me?" said Uncle William. Kendra laughed and gave her uncle a hug as well. "Welcome back to Maple Harbour," he said.

"How was the ceremony?" he asked, as he gave Aunt Jennie a kiss.

All of them spoke at once, talking about the new collection at the museum.

"The Galiano Mask was so cool!" said Kendra. "And a bit scary." Together, they described the grizzly bear mask and the other objects on display in the new wing of the museum.

"I really liked all that old navigation equipment," said Ryan. "And the ships' bells."

"You would love all that maritime stuff, Dad," said Claire to her father. "There are all kinds of old maps and telescopes."

"I certainly intend to go see it for myself," said Uncle William. "Luckily there's no rush. We finally have the collection here in Maple Harbour and it's not going anywhere!"

Aunt Jennie said goodbye and drove off to her other appointment. In the kitchen Uncle William had cut some thick slices of bread and laid out everything they needed to make sandwiches for lunch. There were different types of cheese, ham and salami from the local butcher, and lettuce, tomatoes, cucumbers and peppers from the garden. They each put together a big sandwich and carried it outside to eat on the back deck. Nathan had made a three-layer sandwich and Kendra watched with amusement as he tried to get his mouth around it.

"What are your plans for this afternoon?" asked Uncle William when they had finished their lunch.

"The first thing we should do is go sailing and see how much these guys remember," said Claire, looking at Ryan and Kendra with a grin. "I'm sure you've forgotten everything I taught you."

"Well, maybe not everything," said Ryan. "Now, what's that big stick on the front called?"

"The mast, you dummy!" said Nathan, giving him a friendly shove.

They returned their empty plates to the kitchen and then changed into their swimsuits before making their way to the beach. A rickety set of steps led to a small sandy beach that sloped gently down to the water. The sides of the bay were steep, with twisting reddish-brown arbutus trees clinging to the rocks. In the centre of the bay was a small boathouse and dock. Claire and Nathan called the little bay Pirate Cove, although its official name was Rainy Bay. They all agreed that Pirate Cove was a much better name.

Claire's sailboat was pulled up on the end of the dock. The boat was named *Pegasus*, after the flying horse of ancient Greek mythology. It was a small white dinghy with an aluminum mast, at the top of which fluttered a little blue flag. The flag had a black horse with wings on it. Ryan and Kendra had learned to sail in *Pegasus* the previous year and they couldn't wait to get back out on the water again.

Putting on lifejackets, they raised the sails and slid the boat gently into the water. Meg immediately jumped in, taking her regular spot in the front. Claire steered at first while Ryan and Kendra reacquainted themselves with the various ropes. When they got out of the bay, Claire and Ryan switched places and Ryan took the tiller. He had taken to sailing quickly last year. It was the first sport he'd really enjoyed—although he still wasn't sure if sailing truly counted as a sport.

Tacking back and forth, it didn't take long for Claire's lessons to come back to Ryan. He felt the tug of the tiller as the boat tried to steer into the wind, and he carefully kept it pointed in the right direction. If he steered the boat just right, it moved quickly through the water in spite of the light breeze. Before each tack he was careful to call out a warning so everyone could duck as the boom crossed over their heads.

"I see you haven't forgotten everything I taught you!" said Claire with a big smile. Ryan grinned back.

"Let's just go to that point up ahead," said Claire. "The wind is pretty light and I don't want to get stuck far away if it dies completely."

Ryan steered in the direction she was pointing. When they reached the point, he turned *Pegasus* around, and he and Kendra switched places.

Although Kendra was good at most sports, she wasn't as confident a sailor as Ryan and she sometimes found it difficult to keep the boat on course. Particularly when there were interesting things to look at on shore or in the water and she would forget to keep her eyes on the boat. She tried to remember what Claire had told her about the wind indicators on the sail, but she couldn't recall which way she should turn to keep them straight. So the course they took back was a little wobbly, but she managed to keep them going more or less in the right direction.

Nathan was sitting up in the bow with Meg, who kept trying to lick his face. He had one hand around her neck while his other hand tried to hold onto a book he was reading. Eventually he gave up and, getting to his knees, turned to look out the front of the boat. A few gulls were flying overhead. Off to the left, a seal poked its head out briefly to look at them and then ducked back under the surface. Ahead on the right was a small bay Nathan recognized. He and Claire had sailed in there once. It was quite deep and had an old abandoned wharf, probably part of an old logging operation many years ago.

As he looked toward the shore he saw a dark shadow moving under the surface. It was coming out of the bay and moving toward them. Nathan watched it with interest.

"Hey, what's that?" he said, pointing at the shadow.

"What's what?" said Claire. She and Ryan leaned out to take a look. Kendra, forgetting to watch where she was steering, also turned to look, causing *Pegasus* to veer to the left. She hurriedly sat back and straightened her course.

"That thing under the water. It's moving."

"Is it a fish?" said Ryan.

"It's way too big to be a fish."

"Maybe it's a whale!" said Kendra. Last year they had seen a whale on the last day of their holidays. But there hadn't been any sightings so far this year.

"I don't think so. It's not long enough to be a whale."

Now they could all see it. The object was getting closer, moving quickly toward them under the water. Whatever it was, it appeared to be on a direct collision course with *Pegasus*!

~3~

Bad News

Thinking quickly, Kendra pushed hard on the tiller and the boat swung sharply to the right. But it was too late to get out of the way. By now the object was only a few metres away and *Pegasus* was directly in its path.

They held their breath and waited. But there was no collision. It passed directly under them, several metres below the surface.

"What the heck is that?" said Claire, staring at it. Peering through the water, they could see a red metal structure with two black pontoons sticking out on either side. On the top was a glass dome and they could make out two people sitting inside.

"It's a submarine!" cried Nathan. "Cool!"

"Wow! It really is a sub!" said Kendra. "A mini one!"

"I've seen pictures of them in magazines and on TV," said Ryan. "But I never thought I'd see a real one!"

"Especially passing right underneath us!" said Claire. After the shock of almost being rammed had

"It's a submarine!" cried Nathan.

worn off, her panic had turned to amazement like the others.

"I wonder who owns it." said Nathan. "It came out of that bay with the abandoned wharf, but nobody lives there."

"It probably didn't come from that bay," said Ryan. "When I've read about mini subs like that, they're always launched from a ship of some sort. For doing underwater research and that sort of thing."

Kendra corrected their course and they continued back to Pirate Cove, chattering excitedly about the submarine and what it might be doing around Maple Harbour. Even Meg was caught up in the excitement, wandering back and forth in the boat, wondering what all the fuss was about.

Soon they were back at the dock. They pulled *Pegasus* out of the water and after putting the lifejackets and sails away, they hurried up the stairs to tell Uncle William and Aunt Jennie what they'd seen.

"Guess what we saw!" said Nathan as he ran through the door. "A submarine!"

"Really?" said Uncle William. "I didn't know the navy was doing exercises around here."

"Not a naval submarine. A mini submarine!"

They described the submarine and how it had gone right underneath them. Uncle William and Aunt Jennie were as amazed as they were.

"I've never seen anything like that around here before," said Aunt Jennie. "I wonder what it's doing."

"I think it sounds like a submersible, not a submarine," said Uncle William.

"What's the difference?" asked Ryan.

"Not that much, really. But a submersible is smaller and can only go under water for a short time, while a submarine is self-sufficient and can stay down for long periods of time.

"Anyway, it's a good thing it didn't hit you," he added. "Or I'd have to eat all this lasagna myself!"

Aunt Jennie had just pulled a dish of delicious smelling lasagna out of the oven. They helped to set the table and carried the lasagna into the dining room, along with a big salad full of fresh vegetables from the garden and a loaf of Aunt Jennie's home-baked bread. They sat down to dinner, all of them hungry after a busy day.

"Mmm, I love lasagna," said Kendra, wiping tomato sauce from her face with a napkin. Actually, she liked everything that Aunt Jennie made. Aunt Jennie was a fabulous cook, who seemed able to whip up home-cooked meals every day in spite of her busy job as a village councillor for Maple Harbour.

Over dinner the conversation turned to the ceremony at the museum that morning. Uncle William wanted to know more about what the Galiano Mask looked like. Although he'd heard Aunt Jennie talk about it for many years, he'd never actually seen it.

"It's pretty scary looking," said Kendra. "It's got dark red eyes and a row of sharp teeth."

"It looks ferocious!" said Nathan.

"Well, it's about time that stuff was on display," said Uncle William, as he helped himself to another piece of lasagna.

After dinner, the children went back to the beach to explore the tide pools. The tide was very low, exposing rocky pools filled with mussels, anemones, sea stars, and little hermit crabs scurrying about. Kendra particularly liked to gently touch the sea anemones, which would grip onto her finger with their sticky tentacles. Soon the sun began to set and they returned to the house.

"Time for bed," said Aunt Jennie as they came in. "It's been a busy day and all of you need a good night's sleep."

It certainly had been a very busy first day in Maple Harbour, thought Ryan as he drifted off to sleep.

First the ceremony at the museum and then the excitement of seeing the mini submarine. I wonder what's in store for us tomorrow?

* * *

Sunlight streamed through a gap in the curtains and woke Ryan early the next morning. He threw off the covers and climbed down from the top bunk. Beneath him, Nathan was still sleeping soundly. Quietly getting dressed, he made his way to the kitchen and looked about. Nobody else was around. There was a faint cracking sound outside. He pushed open the kitchen door and stepped onto the porch, squinting in the bright morning sun. He could see Uncle William across the yard, holding an axe high above his head. He brought it down on the piece of wood in front of him, which split apart with a solid crack. Letting go of the axe, he wiped his brow with the back of his glove.

"Good morning!" he called out, seeing Ryan by the door. He waved him over. "You're just in time. I was wondering when my relief crew would arrive." He handed the axe to Ryan and winked. "Ever used one of these before?"

Ryan shook his head. In his house, the fireplace was something that came on when you flicked a switch on the wall. It didn't require any wood to be chopped.

"Well, now's a good time to learn," said his uncle. "This wood splits pretty well. A tree came down on the school grounds this spring and the wood was up for grabs. This is all I could get—free firewood doesn't last long around here." He set a block of wood in front of Ryan and stepped back. "Give it a try."

Ryan looked dubiously at the axe in his hand. This looked like the kind of activity that ended up riding in an ambulance with some toes missing. He raised it hesitantly above his shoulders and brought it down on the block, where it sunk in a couple of centimetres and stuck fast.

"Here, let me show you," Uncle William said, taking back the axe. "First, get it good and high, so the weight of the axe does the work. Second, aim for the edge of the log rather than the centre. That way it's more likely to split." He tapped the spot with the blade of the axe and then handed it back to Ryan.

This time Ryan was determined to have a better attempt. After all, this was Maple Harbour, where last year he had learned to sail, camped on an island, jumped off high cliffs into the ocean, and escaped from criminals in the dark in his bare feet. He raised the axe high above his head and brought it down as hard as he could, exactly on the spot that Uncle William had indicated. There was a loud crack as the log split apart and the two halves flew off to each side. Ryan felt a flush of pride and he turned to look at Uncle William.

"Nicely done!" said his uncle. "Now you can keep going while I get myself a coffee."

Ryan turned back to the wood pile and began to work his way through it. Once he knew how to do it, it was extremely satisfying to feel the wood give way under the blade of the axe. Sometimes the axe got stuck, but more often than not the wood split at least part way through with the first blow and he could finish it off with a second or third. By the time Uncle William came back, Ryan was a good way through the pile of wood, and sweat was pouring down his face.

"That's great," said his uncle, looking at what he'd done. "You can take a break now; pancakes are about to be served."

Ryan set the axe down and followed Uncle William into the house. Inside, the kitchen was a buzz of activity. Kendra was flipping pancakes while Claire was frying bacon and Nathan chopped fruit. Meg was sniffing the floor for crumbs and getting in everyone's way. When she saw Ryan and Uncle William come in, she bounded over to them looking for attention.

Aunt Jennie, who was setting the table, looked up at them as they came in. "You two had better wash up and change," she said, raising her eyebrows. Ryan looked at his shirt, which was streaked with sweat and covered in sawdust. He followed Uncle William to the bathroom to clean up.

When they came back, breakfast was on the table. Nathan carefully stacked his pancakes with layers of bacon before covering it all with maple syrup.

"How can you eat bacon with pancakes?" asked his father.

"They go perfectly together," replied Nathan. "Like peanut butter and marshmallows."

Claire groaned while Uncle William shook his head.

At that moment the telephone rang. Aunt Jennie excused herself and got up to answer it. The others ate their breakfast and talked about what they should do that day. After a few minutes, Aunt Jennie returned. She looked as if she'd just seen a ghost.

Claire looked up at her mother. "What's wrong?" she asked. Aunt Jennie clutched the back of the chair, her hands trembling.

"That was the police," she said. "There's been a break-in at the museum. The Galiano Grizzly Mask has been stolen!"

~4~

Adrift

There was a shocked silence. The four children sat looking at Aunt Jennie, their mouths hanging open.

"What!" exclaimed Uncle William. "Stolen! How?"

The table erupted with questions and exclamations, making such a din that nobody could hear a thing Aunt Jennie was trying to say. Finally, she put her hands in the air and held them up until everyone was quiet.

"I really don't know very much at this point and neither do the police. When the museum staff went to open up this morning, the mask was gone. Apparently someone broke in during the night and stole it. But that's all I know."

The rest of the morning was a bit of a blur for Ryan and Kendra. The phone rang constantly and Aunt Jennie looked very worried. Everyone was asking questions but nobody seemed to have any answers. Eventually Aunt Jennie got into her car and drove to Maple Harbour to speak with the police.

Once she left things settled back to normal. There wasn't anything they could do about the robbery so Uncle William encouraged them to go out sailing in *Pegasus* as they had planned. They began to get ready for a day on the water. They packed sandwiches, snacks, and plenty of water, as well as sunscreen, hats, and extra clothes. It looked like it would be a hot day, but all of them remembered last year, when they had discovered the tunnel on Whalebone Island. That day had started out hot and sunny as well, but ended with them cold and wet after a big thunderstorm.

Ryan went with Uncle William to finish splitting the wood. By the time he finished, the sun was high and the day was already warm. He changed into swim shorts and made his way to the dock, where Kendra and Nathan had put *Pegasus* in the water and were loading it up with gear. As he reached the dock, Ryan had a sudden urge to go for a swim. With a yell, he charged down the dock at full speed and did a cannonball into the water. The others shrieked as the splash soaked them.

"Hey, why'd you do that?" said Nathan, scowling as he rang water out of his shirt. "It's not that hot yet!"

"That's because you haven't been splitting wood all morning," replied Ryan with a grin, and he splashed Nathan again. He then tried to pull himself up onto the dock, but his arms ached from using the axe. "Give me a hand," he called. "I can't pull myself up. My arms are too sore!" But the others just laughed at him and only Meg came over to help by licking his face. Eventually, he swam around to the side of the dock and climbed up the ladder.

"Okay, everybody in," said Claire, untying *Pegasus*. She gave the rope to Kendra and climbed into the back of the boat as Meg jumped in after her. "Oww, get off my foot, Meg!" But Meg had already moved up to the front and was happily looking over the bow.

Once everyone was in, they pushed away from the dock and sailed out to the mouth of Pirate Cove. Kendra and Nathan wanted to go back to Whalebone Island where they had their adventure last year. But the wind was too light and in the wrong direction, so Claire suggested they sail up the coast instead.

It was a beautiful day to be out, with the sun sparkling brightly on the water. The cool breeze on their faces provided a refreshing contrast to the warm sun. Kendra dipped her hand lazily in the water. It was still cool, but it seemed warmer than yesterday. Maybe she'd go for a swim later.

Pegasus hugged the shore as they sailed up the coast. They rounded the headland at the mouth of Pirate Cove. A solitary fir tree was perched on the rocky shore. Beyond was a succession of small coves and beaches, some with a dock or a small cottage in the trees above. In front of one beach they saw the wreck of an old boat with its back end sticking out of the water.

"What's that?" asked Ryan, pointing at it.

"It's an old derelict sailboat that was moored here and then abandoned," said Claire. "One day it broke loose and ended up on the rocks."

"Isn't somebody responsible for it?" asked Kendra.

"No, that's the problem. There's actually no law to prevent you from abandoning a boat. And no one can agree who's responsible for cleaning it up if it sinks."

She steered toward the old wreck. It was covered in barnacles and algae, and the tide was low enough for them to see right through a gaping hole in the hull. Ryan tried to imagine what the boat might have looked like when it was new, with clean white sails and shiny rigging. One thing was clear—it would never sail again.

They sailed past the wreck and around the next point. Ahead of them, perhaps a kilometre offshore, lay a small island.

"What island is that?" asked Kendra.

"It's called Douglas Island. We can go take a look if you like. Although I don't think there's much to see." Claire turned and pointed *Pegasus* toward the island, while Kendra let the sail out in response.

The island began to take form as they got closer. It was quite small and low, not much more than a collection of rocks poking out of the water. In the very middle of the island, a lonely arbutus tree clung to the rocks, its branches gnarled and bent by the wind.

"How can that tree survive out there on those rocks?" said Kendra in amazement.

Ahead and to the left, Ryan thought he could see something floating in the water. It bobbed up and down in the waves, going in and out of view.

"What's that?" he said. The others looked in the direction he was pointing.

"It looks like a boat," said Nathan. "A small dinghy or a canoe."

Claire shifted course again. As they got closer, they could see that Nathan was right. It was a red fibreglass canoe. But it appeared to be abandoned. It was just drifting aimlessly in the sea!

~5~

Tyler

Claire sailed up to the canoe and Nathan reached out and grabbed hold of it. There was a paddle leaning against the seat and a yellow lifejacket lying in the bottom. Otherwise, the canoe was empty.

"Where do you think it came from?" asked Kendra.

"I don't know," said Claire, looking at the canoe thoughtfully. "It looks fairly new, so it couldn't have been abandoned."

Meg, who had been peering into the canoe with her paws hanging over the bow of *Pegasus*, suddenly jumped over the side and into the bottom of the canoe. It rocked dangerously back and forth, and Meg wobbled unsteadily. She sat down and looked at them expectantly.

"She thinks we're going to switch boats and she doesn't want to be left behind!" said Nathan with a laugh.

"Meg, get out of there!" said Claire. "That's not your boat."

Meg looked at her questioningly and stood up on the seat to jump back into *Pegasus*. Then she stopped and her ears perked up. She turned toward the island and gave a little bark. The others turned to look.

Standing on the island by the water's edge, a person was waving their arms in the air. The four of them could just make out the person's faint cries.

"It looks like they're stranded," said Nathan.

"That must be the owner of the canoe," said Claire. "We'd better tow it back to them." She pulled a rope out of the hatch and tied it to the bow of the canoe. Then she wrapped it around a cleat on *Pegasus*.

"You may as well stay in there for the ride, Meg," she said. Meg lay down and stretched out as the canoe began to drift away. As the wind filled the sail, the line drew taut and the canoe followed obediently. They spotted a little patch of sandy beach strewn with seaweed on one side of the island and Claire steered toward it. As they touched ashore, a boy ran along the beach to meet them.

"Thanks a lot!" he said breathlessly. "I was afraid you wouldn't see me here."

"What happened?" asked Claire, untying the canoe from the rope and handing it to him.

The boy grinned sheepishly. "I must have mixed up the direction of the tide," he said, shaking his head. "I thought the tide was going out but it was actually coming in. I was on the other side of the island collecting oysters and when I came back it was gone. That's when I saw your boat and started yelling."

"We didn't hear you. Our dog Meg did," said Nathan, hugging Meg proudly. She licked his ear in response.

"Thanks Meg," said the boy. "You saved me from being stranded here." He patted her on the head.

Kendra looked at the boy curiously. He seemed vaguely familiar to her. Suddenly she remembered.

"You're Tyler, the boy at the museum, aren't you?" she exclaimed.

He looked surprised. "Yes, that's right. Were you there?"

"We all were," said Claire. "Our mom is Jennie Daniels. She's a friend of your grandmother."

The boy smiled broadly. "Oh, I know your mom. She's really nice."

"I'm Claire. And this is my brother Nathan, and our cousins Kendra and Ryan. And this is Meg, but you already met her." Tyler smiled and nodded a greeting.

"Well, thanks again to all of you for bringing my canoe back. It wasn't a very smart thing to do, especially for the son of a fisherman."

"Your dad's a fisherman?" said Kendra.

"No, but my mom is. And my grandfather. And my great grandfather was Captain Phillips, so my family has always worked on the sea here on the coast."

"Our grandfather was a fisherman too, back in Japan," said Ryan.

"And are either of your parents fishermen?"

Kendra giggled. "Not a chance! Dad's a computer programmer. He couldn't catch a fish unless it was in a video game!"

"Well, I may choose to be a computer programmer someday too," said Tyler with a laugh. "I like fishing, but it's hard work if you have to do it every day."

"I guess you heard about the mask being stolen," said Claire.

"Yes," he answered gloomily. "The police were down inspecting the museum this morning, but they don't seem to have any leads. My grandmother is heartbroken about it. After all the work she put into getting it into the museum. In fact, I should probably get back and see how she's doing."

Tyler went back up the beach and returned with a bucket and his shoes, which he dropped into the canoe. Then he pushed it into the water and hopped in.

"Thanks again for bringing my canoe back!" he said.

They waved to him as he paddled off, watching until he disappeared around the island.

* * *

After dinner that evening, the children played Frisbee on the back lawn. Meg was wandering between them, getting in the way and tripping them up as they played. Claire caught the disc and went to throw it to Kendra. As she did so, Meg tried to take it from her and threw her off balance. They all watched as the disc sailed over the hedge and down the embankment to the beach.

Claire groaned. "Meg!" she exclaimed, wagging her finger at the dog.

Kendra went to the gate and looked over. She could see the disc lying on the sand, just above the waterline.

"I'll get it," she called. She walked down the stairs to the beach, with Meg following close behind. As they reached the bottom, Meg suddenly gave a bark and raced ahead. At the end of the dock, Kendra could see someone pulling up in a canoe. It was Tyler! He gave her a wave.

"What are you doing here?" she asked as he tied up to the dock. Meg was busy sniffing around a large white bucket wedged in the front of the canoe.

"I brought you some oysters," he said. He pulled the bucket out of the canoe and placed it on the dock.

"Wow, thanks!" said Kendra, peering into the bucket. It was filled with several dozen oysters. Their shiny white shells were wavy and uneven, each one a slightly different shape. Several of them were encrusted with little barnacles. "I've never had an oyster before."

"Oh, you'll love them," said Tyler. "Or not," he added with a laugh. "Some people like them and some people don't. You'll just have to try them and see."

"I'm sure I'll love them if Aunt Jennie cooks them," said Kendra. "I love everything she makes."

They walked back up the stairs to the house, Kendra stopping to get the disc on the way. Everyone was surprised to see Tyler again so soon.

"Hi Tyler," said Aunt Jennie. "I heard that the kids ran into you on Douglas Island today."

"I brought some oysters as a thank you for finding my canoe." He put the bucket down in front of them.

"Oh, those look wonderful," said Aunt Jennie. "I guess we'll be having oysters for dinner tomorrow!"

"Mmm," said Uncle William, licking his lips.

"Ugh," said Nathan, scrunching up his face. "I hate oysters." Claire glared at him and gave him a jab with her elbow.

But Tyler didn't seem offended. "That's okay. That's what I told Kendra. Some people like them and some people don't."

"Where do you find them?" asked Ryan, gazing into the bucket.

"A few different places. You have to know where they are. But I can show you sometime if you like."

"That would be great!" said Kendra. "I'd love to go oyster hunting. Even if I don't know whether I like them or not."

The others agreed it would be fun to look for oysters. Even Nathan seemed interested. "As long as I don't have to eat them," he said. They arranged to meet the following Saturday. The four of them would sail down to Tyler's grandmother's house in *Pegasus* and then they would all go out together from there.

"You can't miss it. It's the little yellow house with the big arbutus tree in the front yard," he explained. "And maybe we'll dig up some clams," he added. "I know a good place for that too." With a quick wave, he went back through the gate and down to the beach to paddle home.

After Tyler left, the four played some more Frisbee. But it was soon too dark to see, so they turned in. It had been a long day.

Lying in bed, Ryan still felt sore from splitting wood that morning. He wondered if Uncle William felt as sore. How much wood did you need to split before you got used to it and your arms stopped aching?

His mind wandered to Tyler and their upcoming plans to collect oysters. Uncle William sometimes went fishing and would bring home a salmon to barbecue. But Ryan had never heard him talk about harvesting oysters or clams. That certainly wasn't the sort of thing someone could do in the city where he and Kendra lived. He decided he would send a postcard to his grandfather in Japan and tell him about it. Who knows, maybe he'd end up being a fisherman like him one day!

Finders, Keepers

The next few days were rainy and cool, so the four mostly stayed indoors. Claire hated being stuck inside and she moped about, staring out the window. But Kendra and Ryan didn't mind. They liked helping Aunt Jennie and Uncle William with various projects around the house. Uncle William was making a large dining table in his workshop and had a lot of things he needed help with, like cutting pieces of wood, sanding the top, and staining various parts. The table was going to be donated to the local volunteer fire hall. The top was made from a single slab of yellow cedar. It had rough edges like the side of a tree, while the table top itself was polished smooth.

For dinner the next night, Aunt Jennie cooked the oysters Tyler had brought. She baked them in their shells, with lemon juice and herbs. She saved a few for Uncle William to eat raw. Kendra shivered as she watched him slurp them down whole. She wasn't quite sure if she liked oysters or not. They had a funny texture. Ryan liked them though and ate up her share. But they both agreed they weren't going to try them raw, no matter how much Uncle William insisted that was the best way to eat them.

By Saturday the weather had improved and the sun was shining brightly as they set sail for Tyler's place. A light breeze propelled them along and soon they came within sight of the little beach community where Tyler's grandmother lived. As Tyler promised, it was hard to miss the bright yellow house. Right in the middle of the lawn was a big arbutus tree, its peeling orange bark gleaming in the morning sun. They could see Tyler's canoe pulled up on the beach.

He came running down the beach toward them as they pulled in. In his hands he carried a couple of short metal shovels and a white bucket similar to the one he had brought to their house. He dropped them in the canoe and came over to *Pegasus*.

"What are the shovels for?" asked Kendra. "I thought oysters lived on the rocks."

"In case we want to dig for clams," answered Tyler. "There are a few good beaches around for clamming. Who wants to come with me in the canoe?" Ryan volunteered to go with Tyler and the two of them pushed the canoe into the water and hopped in.

"Follow us!" called Tyler as he aimed the canoe toward several rocky islets in the distance. He started to count out their strokes and Ryan kept time, paddling as hard as he could. "One, two, three, four…, one, two, three, four…" Soon they had sweat pouring off their faces and Ryan's arms were starting to ache again. This vacation is going to kill me, he thought wryly.

Meanwhile, *Pegasus* drifted leisurely along behind them. Kendra steered, while Claire and Nathan lazed in the bottom, their feet hanging over the sides. Nathan yelled out encouragement to the boys in the canoe, counting off the paddle strokes with them. Just as they neared the islets, Claire pulled the sail in slightly and *Pegasus* shot past the canoe as they all gave a cheer. Ryan and Tyler slumped over their paddles, exhausted.

The islets were very rocky and there was nowhere to pull *Pegasus* out of the water. So Kendra and Nathan hopped out with their gear while Claire paddled out a bit and dropped the anchor overboard. Then she jumped into the water and swam to shore. They all helped pull the canoe out of the water and onto dry land.

"Where are the oysters?" asked Nathan.

"Over on this side," Tyler answered. They followed him as he crossed the islet to the other side. The tide was very low and there were only a few feet of water between this islet and the next one. Between them, just under the water, the rocks were covered with oysters. They were packed together so tightly that the rocks beneath were scarcely visible, and they had a slightly greenish tinge when looked at through the water.

"Be careful," he said. "It can be pretty slippery, and if you fall the shells are quite sharp." He walked into the water and reached down, pulling up an oyster.

"That's about the size you want," he said, holding the oyster out for them to see. "Not too big, not too small."

"That's it?" said Ryan. "You just wade out there and pick them up?"

"Well, sometimes they stick to the rocks. In that case you can pry them loose or knock them off with a hammer. But there's usually enough of them loose which you can just pick up.

"But that's the easy part. Now we have to shuck it." He pulled a short, sharp knife out of his pack, along with some heavy work gloves. "Hold the oyster with the flat side up and put the knife in the end."

Tyler held the oyster in his hand and stuck the knife between the two halves of the shell. He twisted the knife and wiggled it back and forth until the shell popped open. Opening it up, he pulled the soft fleshy meat from the shell and dropped it into the bucket.

"Some people don't wear gloves, but I always do," said Tyler. "That way I won't cut my hand if the knife slips. And the shells can be pretty sharp."

"Why do we need to shuck them out here?" asked Kendra. "Couldn't we just do it at home?"

"We could. But the shells are important for new oysters to grow on. So it's better to leave them here." Turning, he tossed the shells back into the water.

Claire, Ryan, Kendra, and Nathan all waded into the water and began looking for oysters. Soon they had collected a small pile. Tyler had brought an extra knife and gloves and they took turns trying to shuck the oysters. It was much harder than it looked. Finding a spot to squeeze in the knife was tricky. The oysters were closed tight and didn't want to open.

Ryan seemed to be the best, getting the knack of it quite quickly. Soon he was shucking the oysters almost as fast as Tyler. The others took longer, but after a while they had worked their way through the pile. Inside the bucket was a smaller bucket, which was sitting on a bed of ice cubes. Once they were done, Tyler put a lid on the smaller bucket and then put a towel over the top of the larger bucket to keep them cool and out of the sun.

"Who wants lunch?" said Claire. It was approaching noon and they were all hungry. Claire pulled out the sandwiches and apples that Aunt Jennie had packed and they sat on the rocks munching on them. Tyler pulled out a big tin of smoked salmon to share.

"That's the advantage of having a mom who's a fisherman," he said. "All the smoked salmon you can eat!"

After lunch they were ready for a swim. The sun was high overhead and the day was warm. They clambered over the rocks to where the edge dropped off and plunged into the water. The water felt refreshing after shucking oysters on the hot rocks. They played around in the water, laughing and splashing each other. Nathan swam under the surface and tried to pull Kendra down by her leg, but she was too strong a swimmer for him and he ended up spluttering with his mouth full of water. When they were all tired out, they pulled themselves back up on the rocks to dry off.

"Should we try digging for clams?" asked Tyler. "There's a good beach just over there." He pointed across the water at a long expanse of sand that was exposed by the low tide. The others agreed and, after packing up their things, they set off again in *Pegasus* and the canoe.

The beach was more mud than sand, at least where they landed. Their feet sunk deep into the muck and made a squelching sound with each step they took. Further up the beach the mud turned to sand and they could walk more easily. They dragged the canoe up on the beach, well away from the water.

"I don't want to make the same mistake I did at Douglas Island," said Tyler with a laugh. "I'm going to make sure it can't float away with the tide this time."

Pegasus was too heavy to drag that far up the beach, so again Claire put the anchor out. "At least it won't float away if the tide comes in," she said.

Tyler handed out the shovels and buckets for clam-digging. He showed them how to look for small holes in the sand, which indicated where the clams were buried.

"Watch out they don't squirt you!" he said.

"What do you mean?" asked Nathan. Tyler just shook his head and smiled mysteriously.

It didn't take long to find out. Sometimes the clams would shoot a stream of water up through holes in the sand when they sensed someone was digging for them. One caught Kendra right in the face.

"Ugh!" she cried, wiping the water off her face. Nathan couldn't stop laughing, until another clam squirted all over his shirt. Then it was Kendra's turn to laugh.

They took turns digging as fast as they could to find the clams below. It wasn't as difficult as shucking the oysters, but it was much harder work digging in the hot sun. Many times they came up with nothing after digging a deep hole. Kendra and Nathan soon got bored of digging and began to play Frisbee on the beach. They had brought the disc with them in *Pegasus*, and now they made long passes to each other down the beach.

After a while Claire joined them, leaving only Ryan and Tyler still digging up clams. They played Pig-in-the-Middle, tossing the disc between two of them while the third person tried to intercept it. It was hard to run in the sand, making it difficult for the person in the middle. Eventually Nathan collapsed on the sand after intercepting a pass.

"I can't play anymore," he groaned. He put the disc over his face to hide it from the sun and lay there, panting.

It was hard work digging in the hot sun.

"Let's have a drink," said Claire. "There's lemonade in the boat." She went back down to the boat and pulled the lemonade and some cups out of a cooler they had brought. The lemonade was still nice and cold. They moved to where several large logs were washed up at the high tide line and the three of them sat down on a log and drank their lemonade.

"This is incredible lemonade," said Kendra. "Did Aunt Jennie make it?"

"Yes, she squeezes the lemons herself," said Nathan, shaking his head. "I don't know why she doesn't just use the frozen stuff."

"Because this is way better than frozen lemonade!" exclaimed Kendra. She held out her empty cup to Claire. "More please."

Claire filled Kendra's cup and then put the bottle down beside her on the log. As she passed the cup back to Kendra her elbow bumped the bottle, which wobbled and fell.

"Oops," Claire said and hopped down to retrieve it. As she picked the bottle up and brushed it off, she noticed something glinting in the sand by her feet. She bent down and picked it up.

"What's that?" asked Nathan, looking at the object in her hand.

"It's a watch," she said, peering at it closely. "Oh wow, it's a race watch for sailing!"

"A what?" said Kendra.

"A race watch. It's a special watch designed for sailing races. It counts down the time between flags, and it beeps at the intervals so you can time your start perfectly." She held up the watch for them to see. Kendra couldn't see what made it so special, but it did look expensive.

Nathan rolled his eyes. "You and your sailing races," he said with a smirk. "You've already got a watch!"

"Not one like this. I've always wanted one of these," she said, gazing at it longingly.

"Finders, keepers," said Nathan.

Claire didn't say anything, but continued to examine the watch. Kendra looked at her, a bit surprised. Finders, keepers was the sort of thing Nathan would say, but she thought Claire would know better.

"It may have been here a long time," Claire said after a long silence. "It would be pretty hard to find the owner." She shrugged and put the watch in her pocket and poured herself another glass of lemonade.

Across the beach, Ryan and Tyler had finished digging clams and were walking toward them. They looked hot and tired.

"How many clams did you get?" asked Kendra. They showed her the bucket, which was about half full.

"Not so many," said Tyler. "But enough for a meal."

"Did you leave us any lemonade?" asked Ryan.

"Sure, we saved a bit for you," Claire answered. She poured each of them a cup and handed it to them. Tyler and Ryan hopped up on the log and dangled their feet over the edge, sipping their lemonade.

"Has your grandmother heard anything more about the stolen mask?" Claire asked Tyler.

"No, nothing so far," he replied. "How about your mom? Has she heard anything?"

"No. She's been down to the police station a couple of times but they haven't told her anything new.

"It's pretty strange," she continued. "Mom said that the new wing had a state-of-the-art security system. But no alarms went off."

Tyler thought of his grandmother. When he'd gone by to see her yesterday she seemed very quiet and sad, not like her usual self. The loss of the mask, after so many years of struggling to get it displayed, weighed on her deeply.

"They'd better catch those guys!" he said forcefully. Claire looked at him and then nodded her head in agreement.

After they finished the lemonade, they packed up their things and returned to the boats. It was now late afternoon and they would need to get back if they wanted to be home for dinner. Claire and Kendra paddled the canoe while Tyler went with Ryan and Nathan in *Pegasus*. At Tyler's grandmother's house they dropped Tyler off and helped pull his canoe up on the beach. Tyler insisted they take all the clams and oysters with them.

"We've got lots," he said. He helped push them out and stood on the beach waving as they set sail for home.

"Thanks Tyler," they called, waving back. "We'll see you again soon!"

~7~

A Lucky Find

They all slept in late the next morning. The sun was already high in the sky when Kendra made her way to the kitchen, where Aunt Jennie was chopping up rhubarb and putting it into bags for the freezer.

"Good morning," she said, as Kendra walked in. "You're the first one up. Digging for clams must have worn you all out." Kendra nodded and rubbed her head sleepily.

"Could you please help me chop this rhubarb," continued Aunt Jennie. "A neighbour dropped off a big box of it this morning while you were all sleeping. I'm going to make a rhubarb pie for tonight and freeze the rest."

Kendra took the knife Aunt Jennie handed her and began chopping the rhubarb into small chunks and putting it in the plastic bags.

"Do you kids have any plans for today?" asked Aunt Jennie. "I need a few things from the grocery store, so I thought you might like to ride your bikes into Maple Harbour."

"We can go to Beth's Bakery for cinnamon buns!" said Nathan, who had just walked into the kitchen.

"Ooh, yes!" said Kendra. She remembered going to Beth's Bakery for cinnamon buns last year. They were the best ones she'd ever tasted. Oozing brown sugar and covered in creamy icing. They were to die for, she thought.

By the time they finished chopping the rhubarb, all the children were up. They ate breakfast and washed the dishes, and then set off for Maple Harbour. The old bikes that Uncle William had fixed up for Ryan and Kendra last year were still in the garage. All they needed was some air in the tires and they were off.

They cycled along the winding trail that led to the village of Maple Harbour. The trail was dappled with sunlight poking through the tall fir trees, and the ride was cool and refreshing. After a while the trail joined the road for the last few kilometres into the village. They pulled into the parking lot of the grocery store. Claire went in to pick up the items on Aunt Jennie's list while the others waited outside.

"Got them," Claire said as she came back out. "Now for a cinnamon bun!" She hopped back on her bike and they rode off in the direction of Beth's

Bakery. The bakery was a ramshackle old building with faded wood siding and peeling paint. It had been a summer cottage at one time, but Beth had converted it to a bakery many years ago.

A delicious aroma wafted over them when they opened the big screen door. Kendra breathed in deeply, savouring the smell. It was busy inside and they had to wait in line to order.

"Hi Claire," said the cheerful woman behind the counter. "I see you've got your cousins staying with you again this summer."

"Hi Beth," said Claire. "Yes, they're staying here for a couple of weeks." Ryan and Kendra said hello.

"I trust you won't be dragging them into the sort of adventures you had last year!" she said.

Claire laughed. "We'll try to stay out of trouble."

"I've been waiting all year to come back and have another one of your cinnamon buns," Kendra said as the woman placed the buns onto plates for them.

"Well, I hope they're as good as you remember them," Beth said with a smile as she handed them the plates and their change.

Nathan led the way to a table outside with an umbrella for shade. As they sat down, a tall dark-haired man with a moustache at the table next to them looked up from his paper.

"Hi kids," he said. "I see your cousins are back."

It was Sergeant Sandhu, Maple Harbour's only full-time police officer. Ryan and Kendra greeted him enthusiastically. They had gotten to know Sergeant Sandhu quite well after their adventure with the art thieves the previous year.

"It sounds like you've got another mystery on your hands this summer with the stolen mask," said Ryan.

"Yes," said Sergeant Sandhu, shaking his head. "I'm afraid we're not making much progress on that one."

Claire's face fell. "Really? No clues at all?" she said.

"Well, we figured out how they got inside the museum. The security wiring to one of the back doors had been bypassed. And once they were inside, they were able to disarm the motion sensors. But we have no idea how they bypassed the wiring in the first place. That must have been done during construction. But everything was tested thoroughly before the building opened."

"Hmm, that's strange," said Claire. "I sure hope you catch them. Mom is pretty upset about it, after all that work getting the new wing opened. There's still all the other stuff, but the mask was the highlight of the exhibit."

"Not to mention the most valuable item," added Sergeant Sandhu. "It will be a real shame if we can't find it."

After chatting a bit longer, Sergeant Sandhu went back to reading his paper and the children ate their cinnamon buns. They were warm and gooey, just like Kendra remembered. They ate in silence, licking the icing off their fingers until there wasn't a crumb remaining.

"Mmm, can I have another one?" said Nathan.

"Not a chance," said Claire. "Those cinnamon buns are huge. You'll be ill if you eat two!"

"No I wouldn't!" protested Nathan. Claire rolled her eyes. He was probably right—Nathan could likely eat a dozen of them without getting sick. He had an insatiable appetite for anything sweet.

"We'd better get going and take these groceries back to Mom," she said, standing up. The others followed her out, and they got back on their bikes for the ride home.

They took a different route back than the way they had come, this time winding around the village. Nearing the intersection with the main road, they saw a man come out of a driveway with a sign in one hand and a staple gun in the other. He proceeded to staple the sign to a large pile of lumber at the side of the driveway. Claire slowed down and stopped her bike to read the sign.

FREE LUMBER

"Is that all really free?" she asked.

"You bet," the man said. "They're all leftover pieces from the garage I just finished building. I don't have any need for it, and I don't want it lying around. There are some pretty good pieces in there."

Claire looked at the wood thoughtfully. The others had stopped behind her and were looking at the pile of lumber.

"Why did you stop?" asked Ryan.

"I'm not sure," said Claire. "I'm just wondering what we could do with all this wood."

"Rebuild my fort!" said Nathan. He was thinking of a fort that he and some friends had built in the woods near their house last fall. But they had only had a few pieces of wood and some cedar boughs for a roof. The first wind had knocked it apart. But with a pile of lumber like this, they could build a real fort!

"Or a treehouse?" said Ryan.

"That's it!" said Claire, turning to him with excitement. "We could build a treehouse! There are the remains of an old treehouse in the next bay over from our house. Somebody built it a long time ago, but all that remains is the base. We could use that and build the rest with this wood!"

"Is the base still solid?" asked Ryan.

'I think so. I climbed up there a couple of years ago and it seemed okay. We'll have to check it out, but I think it could work."

Everyone was excited by the idea. "A treehouse is even better than a fort!" said Nathan.

"We'd better get home quickly and ask Dad to pick up this wood with his truck," said Claire. "Before someone else sees it and scoops it."

Getting back on their bikes they sped off, cycling as fast as they could. There was no time to lose!

~8~

Swamped!

"**D**ad, we need your truck!" said Claire, bursting through the front door. She was breathing heavily and still had her bike helmet on.

"I suppose that means you also need me," her father said, looking up from his lunch and raising an eyebrow. "Seeing as you're still a bit young to drive."

Claire looked at him exasperatedly. "Yes, we need you *and* your truck," she said. "Please! We've got to hurry!" She explained quickly about the wood.

"Right, we'd better go," said Uncle William. He was an expert at reusing stuff that people put out for free. Last year he'd found a free chainsaw in almost perfect condition. All it needed was a missing bolt to fix the starter handle. But he knew they had to hurry—free lumber wouldn't stick around Maple Harbour for long!

He grabbed his keys from the counter and ran to the truck with the four children close behind. There was only room for two passengers in the truck, so Claire and Ryan went with him while Kendra and Nathan opted to stay behind.

"Good luck!" said Kendra, crossing her fingers as she waved goodbye.

They drove quickly back down the road to the house where they had seen the free wood. Luckily the lumber was still there. The man who owned the house waved to them from his porch as they began to load the wood into the truck.

The lumber had to be loaded carefully to fit it all in the back of the truck. Uncle William left the tailgate down to get the longer boards in. At last it was all loaded. He tied a red cloth to one of the long pieces, then slowly turned the truck around and began to drive home carefully.

"That's a great find," he said, nodding to Claire and Ryan appreciatively. "I wonder what I can use it for."

Claire and Ryan stared at him. "It's not for you!" Claire burst out. "We're going to build a treehouse with it!"

Uncle William looked crestfallen. "I knew this free lumber sounded too good to be true," he muttered, shaking his head sadly.

When they got home, Kendra and Nathan helped unload the wood and pile it up next to the shed. It was well past lunchtime, so they made themselves some sandwiches while they eagerly explained their plan for a treehouse to Aunt Jennie and Uncle William. As soon as they had eaten, they set off to find the tree and investigate the old platform.

"So where is this tree?" asked Ryan as they walked down the steps to the beach.

"Not too far,' said Claire. "It's in the next bay over from Pirate Cove. You go to the end of the beach and then follow a trail for maybe five minutes."

Just as Claire said, at the end of the beach there was a faint trail that went into the trees. They followed it for a few minutes, climbing up over the headland and down the other side, coming out onto another beach. This beach was longer and more open than Pirate Cove, with pebbles instead of sand. There was a lot of driftwood piled up on the shore which they had to clamber over to get to the beach. Over the years, logs that had escaped from log booms being towed down the coast had washed up on shore, creating piles of driftwood at the top of the beach.

"There it is," said Claire, pointing to a large maple tree a little way down the beach. Sure enough, the remains of an old treehouse could be seen in its lower limbs. There wasn't much left—just a wooden platform that had formed the floor of the treehouse, and part of a wall on one side. They walked over and stood underneath it.

"Wow, this is perfect!" said Kendra. "How do we get up?"

The remains of several old wooden steps could be seen nailed into the tree trunk, but most of them were broken or missing.

"We'll have to climb the tree," said Claire. "I did it before. It's not too bad." She put her foot on one of the remaining steps and then reached up and grabbed a branch above her head. The bark of the tree was smooth, but she was able to get a grip with her shoes and then pull herself up onto the branch. From there it was an easy climb to the platform. The others followed her lead and soon joined her. Meg sat on the ground below and looked up at them forlornly.

"Sorry Meg. You have to stay down there," said Kendra.

"It's quite big," said Nathan. "Someone could sleep up here." He lay back and stretched his arms out over his head. They still didn't reach the other side of the platform.

"As you said, it seems pretty solid," said Ryan, knocking on the wood with his fist. The platform was made of 2x4s, supported underneath by thick wooden beams. Large steel bolts driven into the tree trunk held the beams in place. In the middle of the floor was an opening where the old steps led.

"We'll need to put a hatch cover on that opening," said Claire. "After that, all we need to do is build new walls and a roof."

"Do you think we have enough wood for that?" said Kendra.

"I think so," said Claire. "There's quite a lot of lumber there. And Dad's got some leftover metal roofing he might let us use." They discussed how best to build the treehouse and what pieces of lumber they would need. Claire took measurements of the platform with a tape measure she had borrowed from Uncle William.

"How will we get all the wood here?" said Ryan. "It's not that far, but it's still a long way to carry all that lumber."

Claire thought for a moment. "What if we barge it over on *Pegasus*?" she said. "We'll still have to carry it down to the beach, but that's not too bad."

"That should work. Let's get started!" said Ryan, swinging his legs over the edge to climb down.

"The first thing we should do is build some new steps," said Kendra. "So we don't have to climb up and down like this every time."

"And an elevator for Meg!" said Nathan. Meg, hearing her name, looked up at them and gave a bark. They all laughed, and Meg wagged her tail, greeting each of them as they reached the ground.

* * *

By the time they got back, it was too late to try and bring the wood to the treehouse. Instead they spent the rest of the afternoon organizing the pile and figuring out which pieces they would need and which they could leave behind. Uncle William cut a few of the longer pieces on his table saw and gave them some tools they could use, along with a bag of nails and a rope.

"Take good care of these please," he said.

"We will," they promised.

Just then Aunt Jennie called them to dinner. They trooped into the house, and a delicious smell greeted them as they entered.

"Mmm, is that the rhubarb pie?" said Kendra, raising her nose in the air and breathing deeply.

"It is," answered her aunt as she pulled it out of the oven. They washed up and helped set the table outside for dinner. Aunt Jennie had made roast chicken with mashed potatoes and fresh peas and carrots from the garden. Afterward, she served everyone large slices of pie piled high with ice cream.

"I'm stuffed," said Ryan as he set his fork down and slumped in his chair.

"Well, you need a good meal," said Aunt Jennie. "You've got a busy day tomorrow if you're going to build a treehouse."

* * *

They woke up early the next morning, eager to get going. After gobbling down some toast and cereal they went outside and began to move the lumber down to the dock where it would be transferred onto *Pegasus*. It was hard work carrying the lumber and their initial enthusiasm began to wane after the third or fourth trip. After moving roughly half the pile, they were feeling hot and sweaty and ready for a break. Kendra and Nathan went for a swim while Ryan helped Claire take down *Pegasus'* mast. Since they would be using the little boat as a barge, she wanted all the rigging out of the way. Her plan was to walk in the water close to shore and tow the boat behind them.

After their break, they continued to move the wood until it was all piled up on the dock.

"There, that's it," said Kendra, dropping the last board on the dock.

Ryan and Nathan held *Pegasus* steady while Claire and Kendra carefully placed the wood into the boat. They had to load it carefully so the boat wouldn't tip as they towed it. First, they put all the smaller pieces on the bottom, spreading them around evenly. Then they added the longer pieces, with their ends hanging over the stern. Finally, they laid the metal roofing and some extra pieces of plywood Uncle William had given them on top. Ryan would bring the tools over by way of the trail. That way, if *Pegasus* were to tip, they wouldn't lose all of Uncle William's tools.

"You can hardly see *Pegasus* for all the lumber!" laughed Kendra. Indeed, the little boat was loaded right to the top and it seemed to wobble precariously with any little waves that passed. They carefully pulled the boat around the dock and jumped into the shallow water beside it. With Kendra pulling the rope and Claire and Nathan holding onto the sides, they set off for the next bay.

It was slow going, as they had to step carefully to avoid slipping on the underwater rocks. As they came around the side of the bay, the water got deeper until they could no longer touch the bottom. Kendra hopped up on the shore and made her way along the edge, towing the boat behind her. Claire and Nathan swam along behind, helping to keep the boat away from any rocks. They made their way around the headland until they could touch bottom once more.

"Not much further," said Claire. "We're lucky the water is so calm today."

Kendra looked around. The tide was low and the sea was flat and glassy, broken only by a seal swimming offshore and a motorboat in the distance.

They continued to pull *Pegasus* and the load of lumber toward the shore. Soon they were approaching the beach near the treehouse. Ryan was waiting on shore with Meg. He started to wade into the water to help them, Meg splashing along beside him.

Suddenly, Ryan stopped.

"Look out!" he shouted.

Claire, Kendra, and Nathan turned to look. The motorboat they had seen in the distance had passed by, leaving a large wake behind it. Now it was coming up right behind them!

~9~

The Treehouse

The three children jumped out of the way just as the wave hit. It crashed into *Pegasus*, raising the little boat up and tipping it over sideways toward the shore. All the wood poured out into the sea!

The four looked at each other, their mouths open in shock. Then Claire started laughing.

"Oh well, now we don't have to unload it!" she said, picking up a piece of wood floating nearby.

The others laughed with her when they realized that they hadn't lost any wood—it just had to be carried up to the beach. The boat righted itself quickly and Ryan took the bow line and pulled it up onto the beach. Some of the wood had already washed up so they began to collect the pieces that were still floating in the water. Even Meg helped, happily carrying pieces of wood in her mouth and adding them to the pile. Kendra found the sheets of metal roofing nearby where they had sunk to the bottom. She picked them up and carried them ashore. When they'd managed to recover all the spilled wood, they sat down to have a break.

The wave tipped Pegasus over sideways.

"Hey look, there's Tyler!" said Kendra, pointing out across the water. Sure enough, the little red canoe was paddling across the mouth of the bay. She gave a shout and Tyler turned the canoe and paddled toward the beach.

"Hi there," he said, hopping out of the canoe. "I was just going to paddle by your house and see if you were there. What are you doing here?" He looked at the pile of wood on the beach.

They explained about finding the free wood and their plans to build a treehouse.

"Do you want to help?" asked Claire.

"Sure!" said Tyler.

"We've done most of the hard work, getting the wood here," joked Nathan. "So you can just move it the rest of the way while we take a break." Tyler looked at the pile dubiously.

"Just ignore him," said Claire. "It will go quickly with five of us."

She was right. Together they were able to get the wood moved over to the base of the tree in no time. Now they could start building the treehouse.

Their first task was to replace the ladder so they could get up the tree easily. Kendra and Nathan nailed some prc-cut 2x4s onto the trunk of the tree. The first few were easy but the higher ones were more difficult to nail in, as they had to hang on with one hand while hammering with the other. But soon they had a full set of steps up to the opening in the floor.

Meanwhile, Ryan climbed up to the platform and tied a pulley to a large, solid branch. Tyler threw a rope up to him and he tied it around the branch. Then Tyler pulled the other end through another pulley with a large steel clip on it. He tossed the rope up to Ryan, who looped it through the first pulley. Now they would be able to hoist heavy loads up to the platform using the pulleys instead of having to carry them up the ladder.

Claire was busy taking measurements and laying out pieces of lumber. The plan was to build the walls down below and then pull them up and nail them onto the platform. She carefully measured each piece of wood and marked it with a line where it needed to be cut.

When she was done, they each took turns cutting. A large rock near the base of the tree made a good workbench. They started off enthusiastically, but it was slow work as they only had a hand saw to cut with. Each piece took longer than the last to cut.

Claire watched irritably as Nathan sawed through his piece. There was a growing stack of wood waiting to be cut. Nathan stopped and rested. He was only about a third of the way through.

"Hey, no stopping!" said Claire. "There are lots of pieces waiting to be cut."

Nathan groaned and started sawing back and forth again. But he soon stopped again. Now he was about halfway through.

"Ryan, you cut it for him," sighed Claire. Ryan, who was holding the piece of wood steady on the rock, let go and moved to take the saw. But Nathan held onto the saw and started cutting again furiously. Without anyone to hold it, the piece of lumber swung around and fell off the rock, landing on Meg! She gave a little squeal and jumped out of the way.

"You idiot!" yelled Nathan. "Why did you let go?" He rushed over to Meg and threw his arms around her. Meg, who seemed none the worse for wear, licked his face happily.

"Sorry," said Ryan. "I didn't know you were going to start sawing again." He felt guilty about letting the board hit Meg, but he didn't really think it was his fault.

"Well, don't think you know everything and can just take over!" Nathan said as he stormed off down the beach with Meg following behind him. Everyone stared after him.

"Sorry," said Claire. "That was my fault."

They continued to cut the pieces of wood to length, but everyone was more subdued now. Ryan kept glancing down the beach to see if Nathan would return. He knew it wasn't really his fault, but he felt bad nonetheless.

Suddenly, Nathan and Meg reappeared by the tree.

"Hey, guess what we found!" he said excitedly. He seemed to have forgotten all about being upset. "Something in the water! Come and take a look!"

The others scrambled to their feet and followed Nathan onto the beach. He pointed to a dark shape in the water in front of them. They waded in to get a closer look.

A few centimetres below the surface they could see a metal frame with rusting gears and shafts, and a round tank at the top. A section of the tank had been torn away, leaving a sharp jagged edge sticking up.

"What is it?" asked Kendra.

"It's an old piece of machinery of some sort," said Claire. "Maybe a donkey engine left over from an old logging operation." She stepped a little closer, although still keeping some distance. "It looks pretty dangerous though. Someone could cut themselves on those sharp edges. We should be careful to stay well away from it."

They waded to shore and walked back to the treehouse. Nathan sidled up to Ryan as they walked.

"Sorry about what I said," Nathan muttered quietly. "I know it wasn't your fault."

'It sort of was," said Ryan. "I shouldn't have let go of the wood."

"It was really Claire's fault," said Nathan, raising his voice so Claire could hear them. He pretended to glare at her and then laughed.

She laughed back. "I guess that's what older sisters are for," she said. "To take the blame for everything. Anyway, it's a good thing you're back because it's your turn to cut again."

They went back to cutting the pieces with fresh energy now that Nathan had returned. Soon all the pieces were cut and they began to nail them together. They made a frame for the wall and then nailed thinner pieces of wood on the outside to cover it, remembering to leave space for a window. When they were done, they stood it up to admire their work.

"It looks pretty good!" said Kendra. Some of the pieces didn't quite join together perfectly and there were a few bent nails, but overall it looked sturdy.

Ryan tried to lift it. "Ugh, it's pretty heavy," he said. "But I think we should be able to get it up there with our pulley system."

He and Tyler carried it over to where the rope dangled from the tree. They tied a piece of rope around the wall section and attached it to a clip on the end of the pulley. Then they both pulled on the loose end of the rope.

"Wait," said Kendra. She, Claire, and Nathan climbed up the ladder to the treehouse. The section of wall rose in the air toward them. When it reached the top, they pulled it over and onto the platform. Then they manoeuvred it into place and nailed it to the floor.

"Hooray!" they all cheered together. "One wall done, three more to go."

They had done a lot that morning and it was well past noon. Nathan's stomach was growling, so they walked back home to get some lunch. Aunt Jennie greeted them as they came in.

"I'm surprised Nathan has survived this long without any lunch," she said, glancing at the clock. She pulled a big dish of homemade macaroni and cheese out of the oven and set it on the table. The five children wolfed it down hungrily. Afterward, they cut up a watermelon and sat on the lawn to eat it. Their stomachs full, they lay back on the grass, soaking up the warm sun.

"Let's just lie here all afternoon," said Ryan, shading his eyes against the sun. "I could easily fall asleep."

"Come on you lazybones," said Claire. "We've got three walls and a roof to build."

They slowly got to their feet and got ready to go back to the treehouse. Tyler called his mom to let her know that he wouldn't be back until dinnertime. They filled up a big jug of water to take with them and returned to work.

The other walls seemed easier now they had finished the first one. Their cuts were straighter and there were fewer bent nails. One by one they assembled the walls and pulled them up to the platform. Once the walls were up, they lay some boards over top as a roof and nailed the metal roofing in place. One wall was built higher than the others so the roof sloped down to one side.

Each wall had a window opening so they could see out in all directions. Facing west they could just see the beach through the trees. The other windows faced into the forest. Tyler looked out one of the windows and was surprised to see a squirrel looking straight back at him from a branch on the next tree.

On the side near the rope and pulley there was an opening for a small door so they could still haul supplies up that way.

It smelled of fresh cut wood inside. There was lots of room to move around, and they could kneel without hitting their heads on the roof. Kendra put a few nails into the walls to hang things on, making sure to place them high enough so no one would hit their head.

"Now we just have to make some shutters and a hatch cover for the opening in the floor," said Claire as they sat in the treehouse and drank some of the water they had brought.

It didn't take long to cut the boards to make window shutters. For the door they used two boards side by side and nailed several smaller pieces across to hold them together. Ryan found a piece of plywood that was just the right size for a hatch cover.

"Oh, no," groaned Claire as she fitted the hatch cover over the opening. "We don't have any hinges."

The others looked at her in disappointment.

"Does Uncle William have any?" asked Kendra.

"I don't think so," said Nathan. "He used a hinge to fix Mom's sewing chest last week, and I remember him saying it was the last one he had."

"We need them for the shutters too," said Claire. "We'll have to go to the hardware store tomorrow and buy some. It's too late to go into the village today."

While they were disappointed to have not finished the treehouse, they were proud of the progress they had made. Their own treehouse! As they packed up the tools, Kendra looked up at it in the branches above them. The afternoon sun was shining on it through the trees, giving it a warm glow. It looks just like a treehouse should look, she thought to herself with satisfaction.

~10~

Ice Cream

After downing a large breakfast of bacon and eggs with toast and jam, they set off on their bikes the next morning for Maple Harbour.

"Take heart, kids. It wouldn't be a real construction project without a trip to MBS to pick up something you forgot," said Uncle William as they left. MBS stood for Maple Building Supplies, a place where Claire swore her dad spent half his time picking up tools and materials.

MBS was across from the grocery store. They pulled into the parking lot and leaned their bikes against the wall. Inside the store was busy with people picking up lumber, paint, and tools for their summer construction projects. The aisles were filled to the ceiling with every possible type of hardware and tool needed for building. There were shelves full of screws and nails, light sockets and switches, showerheads and paint brushes. The children stood near the entrance, unsure of where to start.

"Can I help you find anything?" asked a friendly young woman standing nearby.

"We're looking for hinges for our treehouse," said Claire.

"Sure, no problem. They're over here." She led them down one of the aisles where they saw a shelf filled with plastic containers holding hinges of all sizes and styles. They picked through them, looking for the ones that would best suit their purpose.

"How about these?" said Ryan, holding up a pair of ornate gold hinges with beautiful spirals on them.

"Or these," said Nathan, picking up a huge pair of black steel hinges, so heavy he had trouble lifting them. "I think these are meant for a castle drawbridge!"

Claire laughed. "I think we can make do with these," she said, pulling a dozen or so small, basic hinges out of a box. "Now we need screws."

They made their way to the next aisle to look for screws. Nathan spied something at the back of the store and wandered off to take a look. When he rejoined them, he was carrying a shopping bag and looking pleased with himself.

"What did you buy?" asked Kendra.

"It's a surprise," he said, holding the bag tightly.

They waited in line to pay for the hinges and screws. The teenage boy working at the till greeted Claire. She knew him vaguely through some of the sailing races. His uncle had a boat and the boy sometimes came with him to help out.

"Have you seen the yacht in the harbour?" the boy asked, as he scanned their items through the till. Claire shook her head.

"You should check it out," he continued. "It's pretty amazing. It's absolutely massive and must have cost millions. It's even got a little submersible on the back."

"Really? A sub?" said Ryan, glancing at Claire. She was listening with interest.

"Yup, a real sub. Apparently the guy who owns it is some kind of scientist. His crew are all marine biologists. They're on some kind of expedition to study the marine life here."

Claire paid for the hinges and screws and they went outside.

"That must be the sub we saw the other day!" she said.

"Let's go check it out!" said Nathan. Grabbing their bikes, they rode to the harbour and onto the wharf. The wharf was at the end of the main street. It was made of large timbers, and their bicycles bounced roughly over them as they rode. It wasn't hard to spot the yacht the boy had been talking about. It was moored at the very end of the wharf and towered over all the other boats.

The yacht was very sleek, with darkly polished teak rails and gleaming chrome trim. It was three levels high, with a huge sundeck extending from the back of the upper level. An elderly man with grey hair sat in a lounge chair on the sundeck. He was wearing a navy blue polo shirt and dark sunglasses, and was reading some papers. A laptop sat on the table beside him.

"Do you think that's the owner?" whispered Kendra.

"Must be," said Claire. "Maybe he was the one driving the sub when we saw it."

They wandered to the stern of the boat and stared up at the submersible suspended from a crane. It was a very small submersible, only big enough to hold two people. It was bright red, with two large black tanks on the sides. A large clear plastic bubble surrounded the cockpit, and they could see the dials and controls inside.

A young man with blonde hair and long side-burns came out on the deck and smiled down at them. He was wearing white shorts and the same style of navy blue polo shirt as the older man.

"You like our sub?" he asked them.

"It's so cool!" said Nathan enthusiastically. "Do you take people for rides?"

The man laughed and shook his head. "Sorry, crew only."

"What do you use it for?" asked Ryan.

"Exploring marine life where it's too deep to dive. This thing can go down to 300 metres," he explained. "We're on a research expedition right now."

"What are you researching?" asked Ryan. He was very interested in marine life.

"Starfish," said the man. "There's a disease that's killing them off. We're researching why that's happening." Suddenly, there was a call from inside the cabin. "Sorry, I've got to go," he said, turning to leave them.

They wandered back to where they had left their bikes. Ryan looked puzzled.

"What's wrong?" asked Kendra, who could tell when something was bothering her brother.

"Oh, nothing," he said, shaking his head. Kendra looked at him curiously, but Ryan didn't say anything more.

* * *

"What time is it?" asked Nathan as he got onto his bike.

"10:32," Claire said, looking at her wrist.

"Perfect, we have time to go for ice cream," said Nathan.

"Good idea," said Ryan.

Kendra noticed Claire was wearing the watch that she had found on the beach the other day. She looked away awkwardly when she saw Kendra staring at it.

It was only a couple of blocks along the waterfront to the ice cream shop. They leaned their bikes against the side of the building and entered the store. A bell tinkled as the door swung open. The owner looked up.

"Nathan!" said a woman behind the counter. "Never too early for ice cream, eh?" Nathan grinned shyly. Although he didn't know the store owner's name, he obviously came here often enough that she knew his!

There were dozens of flavours to choose from. They walked back and forth in front of the display cases, pondering their choices. The owner gave them samples of the newest flavours to try before they eventually made up their minds. They paid for their cones and went outside to eat them, sitting at a small table in front of the store.

Kendra thought the ice cream shop in Maple Harbour had the best ice cream in the world. She had a raspberry cheesecake ice cream cone, with whole raspberries and a creamy, cheesy, flavour. Claire had chosen chocolate orange while Ryan had key lime pie. Nathan's cone was a very dark brown, almost black.

"What flavour is that?" Kendra asked. "Caramel?"

"Nope. Root beer!" he said, giving it a big lick.

When they finished their ice cream they went around to the side of the store to get their bikes. But when they got there, they stopped short and stared.

"My tires are flat!" said Ryan, looking at his bike in dismay.

"So are mine!" cried Kendra and Nathan together.

In fact, the tires on all four bikes were completely flat. There was laughter above them and they looked up. The Mitchell brothers, Matthew and Flint, were leaning over a railing on the road above, sneering at them. As usual, the troublesome twins were dressed identically, wearing green polo shirts and khaki shorts.

"Good thing it's a FLAT ride home!" called Matthew. He doubled over laughing at his own joke and gave his brother a high five. Then they disappeared from view.

Nathan was furious. He started to give chase, but realized the only way up to the road above was by going all the way to the end of the block and around. By then the Mitchells would be long gone. Besides, what could he do? The Mitchells were older, bigger, and faster than any of them.

Luckily, Claire had a small pump on her bike. But it took a long time to reinflate all eight tires.

"I'll need another ice cream after this," said Nathan as he pumped his tires.

"No you don't," said Claire. "We need to get back and finish our treehouse."

"Those rotten Mitchells! What can we do to get back at them?" said Kendra, thinking back to last year when they had tried to dump a rotting salmon in the Mitchells' boat before being caught in the act.

Claire didn't answer. She'd been oddly silent since seeing the Mitchells. As Matthew was leaning over the railing laughing, she'd noticed he was wearing the exact same watch as she was, the one she had found on the beach. But Flint wasn't wearing any watch at all.

~11~

Stormy Weather

Nathan was still angry at the Mitchells when they got back. He explained to his mother and father what had happened. Uncle William just laughed.

"Boys will be boys," he said.

Nathan glared at him. "See if you like it if they let the air out of your truck tires!"

His mother smiled sympathetically and pushed a plate with a large ham and cheese sandwich across the counter. Nathan picked it up hungrily and began to eat. Soon he had calmed down, and by the time he finished he had completely forgotten about the Mitchells.

"Let's go finish the treehouse!" he said, jumping up.

The others were still eating their sandwiches. Aunt Jennie handed Nathan a large bowl filled with plump red cherries. "Have some fruit," she said. Nathan took the bowl to the back deck and ate the cherries, seeing how far he could spit the pits across the lawn. The others joined him and soon they were all competing for the farthest cherry pit spit.

"I win!" said Ryan as one of his pits sailed all the way across the lawn and into the flower garden.

"Now we'll get a new cherry tree growing there," laughed Claire.

When the cherries were gone, they gathered their tools and set off for the treehouse. It didn't take long to screw the hinges onto the hatch and shutters and put them in place in the treehouse. Soon they were finished.

"Hooray, we're done!" said Kendra, sticking her head out a window and looking down at the others below.

"Not quite," said Nathan. He opened his pack and pulled out the shopping bag he had picked up that morning at MBS. Opening it up, he pulled out a strange looking object. It was made of orange cloth with all sorts of straps and clips attached to it.

"What's that?" asked Ryan.

"It's a dog harness." He whistled and Meg came running over from the beach where she had been sniffing under some logs. She stood obediently at his side while he put the harness over her head and did up the straps.

"Or to be more accurate," he said, "it's a dog elevator!"

"You're not serious, are you?" said Claire. "Meg will never go up in that."

"Sure she will. You saw her watching us the whole time we were building the treehouse. She was dying to get up there." He led Meg over to the rope and pulley, and clipped the pulley to a sturdy handle on the top of the harness. Meg looked at him expectantly.

"Somebody help me pull," he said. Ryan took hold of the rope while Claire looked on dubiously. Together they began to slowly hoist her up. Meg looked surprised as she suddenly rose into the air. She turned her head from side to side, wondering what was happening.

"Hi Meg!" called Kendra, sticking her head out through the little access door. Meg looked up at her and wagged her tail. When she was level with the treehouse Kendra swung her over and through the door. She unclipped the rope while Claire, Ryan, and Nathan scrambled up the ladder.

Inside, Meg was excited to be up in the treehouse. So this was where they had all been while she was left

Meg looked surprised as she suddenly rose into the air.

waiting on the ground below! She sniffed each corner of the treehouse and then circled a few times before lying down happily.

"Way to go Meg!" said Nathan. "You're a flying dog now!"

They petted and hugged Meg, happy to have her with them. It hadn't seemed right to be up in the treehouse with Meg stranded down below. Now they could all be together!

* * *

When they got home, Aunt Jennie quickly put them to work peeling potatoes and chopping vegetables. After they finished, she gave them popsicles from the freezer. Aunt Jennie's popsicles were always made from a mystery mix of fruits and juices, with the occasional vegetable thrown in. The children wandered outside, licking their popsicles and trying to guess what was in them.

"Bananas," they all agreed.

"And strawberries," said Ryan. "They must have something red in them to be this colour."

"No, I think it's cherries," said Kendra. "I saw her putting them in the blender this morning."

"I'm pretty sure I can taste broccoli," said Nathan.

"How would you know?" said Claire, laughing. "You never eat your broccoli!"

Outside the sky was starting to cloud over and a breeze was picking up. Kendra reached out to grab her napkin, which had suddenly blown away from her.

"Hmm, looks like a storm might be coming," said Claire, eyeing the clouds. The weather had been very calm since Ryan and Kendra arrived, with only a light breeze at times and often no wind at all. Uncle William, who had just stepped out the back door to light the barbecue, overheard her.

"I think you're right," he said, looking at the sky. "Better make sure everything is put away."

They checked around the yard to make sure nothing would blow away or get rained on. Claire went down to the beach to make sure *Pegasus* was pulled up on the dock and securely tied down. By this time the wind had picked up and the temperature had dropped several degrees.

"I guess we won't be eating outside tonight," said Aunt Jennie. Instead she had them set the table indoors. Uncle William brought in a big dish of barbecued chicken and they sat down to eat. There were roast potatoes and vegetables, freshly baked rolls, and a big salad loaded with lettuce, carrots, and cucumbers from the garden and tomatoes from the greenhouse. Just when Ryan thought he couldn't eat another bite, Aunt Jennie came out with another pie.

"Is that rhubarb pie again?" asked Uncle William as she handed him a piece.

"Yes, it is. There was a lot of rhubarb, so you're getting rhubarb pie two nights in a row."

"Mmm, I could eat it every night," Ryan said, tucking into the pie.

By the time they finished dinner, the trees outside were swaying wildly in the wind. They played cards around the kitchen table. Uncle William was winning, which was unusual, as normally Claire won when the family played cards. But tonight she had trouble concentrating.

"Claire, pay attention!" said Nathan, as Claire placed a card down on the pile. "I know you have an ace—you just took it from me!"

Claire looked at her cards. "Oh yeah, so I do." She took the card from her hand.

"Too late!" said Uncle William, picking the card off the table. "I'm out!"

Nathan groaned and picked up the cards to deal another hand. Outside the wind whistled and the branches of the trees whipped back and forth. After a while it began to rain and the wind blew raindrops against the windows. The lights flickered and dimmed before coming back on.

"There might be a power outage," said Uncle William. As he spoke the lights flickered again. A moment later they went out altogether.

Aunt Jennie lit several candles and they tried to continue playing. But it was hard to make out the cards in the dim candlelight. When Kendra began to yawn, they gave up and went to bed.

* * *

Kendra woke in the middle of the night. The wind outside was howling and she felt the whole house shake. She looked at the clock but it was dark. The power is still out, she thought.

She heard Claire stir in the bed on the other side of the room. "Are you awake?" she whispered.

"Yes," said Claire. "The shaking of the house woke me up."

"Me too."

Claire got up and opened the curtains. It had stopped raining and the moon was out. The trees swayed and bent wildly in the storm. Claire opened the window briefly and the wind rushed in, blowing papers off her desk and scattering them around the room. She quickly closed it and climbed back into bed.

They lay there in silence for a while, listening to the storm. After a while Claire spoke.

"Do you think I should keep that watch?"

So that's what's been bothering her, thought Kendra. Ever since they had come back from Maple Harbour yesterday, Claire had seemed distracted and lost in her thoughts.

"I don't know. What do you think?"

Claire didn't reply.

"I suppose it's kind of hard to return it if you don't know who it belongs to," said Kendra. "Maybe you could put up a sign or something."

"I think I know whose it is."

"Really? Who?"

"Flint Mitchell."

Kendra groaned. "Oh, well, in that case …"

"I know," said Claire. "If anyone deserves to lose a nice watch, it's one of the Mitchell brothers." She explained how she'd seen Matthew in the village wearing the same watch, but not Flint. "And they always have the same of everything."

Kendra turned over and looked at Claire. She could see her profile clearly in the moonlight.

"So instead of getting back at them for letting the air out of our tires, you're going to give him back his watch?"

"I think I have to," she said glumly. "It's the right thing to do."

Kendra sighed and nodded. "I guess you're right." The Flint brothers might be awful, but it still wasn't right to hang onto their watch.

The wind continued to howl and the house shook violently again.

Kendra shuddered. "It feels like the whole house is going to blow away."

Just then, there was an awful cracking sound, followed by a huge crash!

~12~

Lost Property

Claire and Kendra jumped out of bed and ran to the window. They looked outside but couldn't see anything. They heard footsteps in the hallway and rushed out, nearly bumping into Uncle William as he hurried past. With the girls close behind, Uncle William ran to the front door and opened it.

"Oh no," he groaned. Across the lawn they could see his truck in the moonlight. A large tree branch had fallen on it, putting a huge dent in the roof!

"Oh, Dad, I'm so sorry," Claire said, putting her arm around him and giving him a hug.

Aunt Jennie, Ryan, and Nathan were standing behind them now, staring out the door. Nobody said anything. Everyone knew how attached Uncle William was to his truck.

"Oh, well," Uncle William said at last. "It was time for a new truck anyway." He turned and looked at them, a big smile on his face. "Just last week I noticed the trucks at Coastal Motors and was thinking I might be in need of a new one."

"But you loved that truck!" protested Nathan. "You always said you loved it more than your family!"

"And I'll love the new one even more," Uncle William said with a gleam in his eyes.

There was nothing more they could do until morning, so they went back to bed. But it was already beginning to get light and nobody could fall back asleep. Soon they were all gathered in the kitchen, eating an early breakfast.

"I'm going to go into town and talk to the insurance agent as soon as they're open," said Uncle William as he made himself a coffee. "I suspect they may be busy today."

"Can I come with you?" said Claire. "I have a few things I want to do."

Kendra glanced at her, but Claire's face gave nothing away.

Shortly after eight o'clock, Claire and her father headed into town in Aunt Jennie's car. They pulled into a parking space in front of the insurance agency and Uncle William went in to file a claim for his truck. Claire walked down the street, stopping in front of a glass door next to a clothing store. On the door it said *D. A. Mitchell – Solicitor*. Claire took a deep breath and turned the handle.

Inside, a set of stairs led to an office. A receptionist looked up from behind a large desk.

"Is Mr. Mitchell in?" asked Claire.

The receptionist nodded and picked up the phone. A moment later a door opened and Matthew and Flint's father came out. He was a big burly man with a bushy moustache. Mr. Mitchell greeted her warmly.

"Good morning, Claire. What brings you in today?"

Claire fished the watch out of her pocket and held it up. "Is this Flint's watch?" she said, secretly hoping she was wrong.

Mr. Mitchell looked at it in amazement. "Well, I'll be. It is indeed. We'd given up on finding it. It's been lost for weeks. Those watches were gifts from their grandmother last Christmas, and I was furious with Flint for losing it. Where did you find it?"

Claire explained how she'd found it on the beach behind the log. She handed it over to Mr. Mitchell.

"Well you're in luck," he said. "You can give it to him yourself. The boys are here doing some paperwork for me." Claire groaned inwardly. She had hoped to avoid Matthew and Flint, which is why she'd come here instead of going to their house.

Mr. Mitchell opened the door to a small side office and called the boys out. Matthew and Flint emerged from the room, pushing and shoving each other as they came through the door. When they saw Claire they stopped short.

"It wasn't a big deal. We just …" Matthew started to say, but his father stopped him with a stern look.

They think I'm here to complain about letting the air out of our tires, thought Claire.

Mr. Mitchell held up the watch and Flint gasped. "Claire found this on the beach. She recognized it as yours and came here to return it. Not that I'm sure you deserve it," he muttered under his breath.

Flint took the watch from his father and looked at it. Then he looked at Claire. "Thanks," he mumbled. "Sorry about your bikes." His father gave him a sharp look.

"It's no problem," said Claire. "It belongs to you." She was already turning to go.

Mr. Mitchell walked down the stairs with her and held the door.

"I'm sorry for whatever those boys did lately," he sighed. "I probably don't want to know." Claire laughed.

"It's nice to know there are kids like you out there who always do the right thing." He held out his hand and Claire shook it.

She said goodbye and stepped out onto the sidewalk, blinking in the bright light. The sun was out and the day was warming up quickly now the storm was over. Glancing around she noticed two expensive looking bikes locked to a bike rack across the street. Those look familiar, she thought.

She walked across the street and looked at them more closely. They were identical bright yellow mountain bikes. One of them had a small repair kit strapped under the seat, with the name *F. Mitchell* written on it.

Claire looked around. There was nobody nearby. It would be easy enough to let the air out of their tires and get even with the Mitchell boys.

Claire thought about what Mr. Mitchell had said. That she was someone who would 'always do the right thing.' Sometimes she wished that wasn't the case. Just once she would like to do something really mean and nasty to the Mitchells. But she just couldn't bring herself to do it.

I guess being nice isn't such a bad thing, she thought with a grin. Turning, she walked away from the bikes and hurried back to find her dad.

* * *

When Claire got back to the insurance agency, she could see her dad was still waiting in line for an agent. His hunch that the wind storm would result in a lot of insurance claims was obviously correct.

She decided to wander down to the harbour to kill some time. Stopping at the marina, she poked her head in the door.

"Hi Claire," a grey-haired man with bushy eyebrows said to her. He was rearranging fishing lures for sale on the wall. "Every day I have to re-organize these lures," he grumbled. "You'd think people could put them back in the same place after looking at them."

"Hi George," said Claire. "You wouldn't have anything to do all day if everything was in order," she joked.

"I suppose that's true," he said, laughing.

"Did the storm do any damage here?" she asked.

"A little bit, but nothing too bad. One boat lost a dinghy and another had a torn sail cover. How about yourselves?"

Claire told him about Uncle William's truck. He shook his head sympathetically.

"Any damage to the big yacht?" she asked.

"No, a big boat like that isn't troubled too much by that storm," said George, shaking his head. "But it looks like they're getting ready to leave."

"I heard the owner is a scientist and they are on some sort of research expedition."

"Retired scientist," he corrected her. "His name is Robert Borman. He comes from a wealthy East Coast family. But I gather he prefers to live on his yacht here on the West Coast, doing his own research."

Saying goodbye to George, Claire continued her walk around the harbour. The big yacht was still moored at the end of the wharf. She walked down to take another look. A pickup truck was parked on the wharf, its back filled with groceries and supplies. A delivery driver was handing up boxes to a crew member on the deck of the yacht. As George had mentioned, it looked like they were getting ready to leave.

As she watched, a cabin door opened and a man stepped out carrying a backpack over one shoulder. He walked to the front of the yacht and then down the gangplank onto the wharf. As he got closer, Claire recognized the man as Jim Jenson, the museum curator.

"Hi Mr. Jenson," she said as he walked by. The man jumped, looking startled.

"Oh, hello Claire." He pushed his hair back with one hand. "What are you doing here?"

"I'm just waiting for my dad." She explained about Uncle William's truck. "Have you had any more news from the police about the break-in at the museum?" she asked.

Looking down at the wharf, he shook his head sadly. "No, I don't suppose we'll ever see that mask again."

"Don't say that! Thieves always get caught in the end!"

Jim Jenson looked at her curiously, his head tilted to one side. "Perhaps you're right," he said. "Anyway, I must be going. There are still plenty of artifacts left to look after at the museum." Gripping his backpack tightly, he strode off down the wharf.

When Claire got back to the insurance agency, Uncle William was just coming out, looking very pleased.

"They'll have to take a look at it," he said. "But it's almost certainly a write-off. And they'll give me quite a bit more for it than I was expecting."

As they drove home, Uncle William talked excitedly about all the features he was looking for in a new truck. Claire looked out the window, not paying much attention. She wasn't very interested in cars or trucks. She was much more interested in boats!

When they got home, Aunt Jennie told them that Ryan, Kendra, and Nathan had taken Meg and gone to the treehouse.

Claire was hungry since she'd eaten breakfast so early that morning. She made herself a piece of toast from a fresh loaf of bread that Aunt Jennie had baked. Then she planned to get changed and go look for the others.

Just as she was finishing her toast, Meg burst through the open front door and skidded to a stop in front of her. She was followed immediately by Nathan, Kendra, and Ryan.

"We've had a brilliant idea!" said Nathan, trying to catch his breath. "We're going to sleep in the treehouse tonight!"

A Night in the Treehouse

Aunt Jennie looked at Nathan, her eyebrows raised.

"In the treehouse?" she said. "Will you all fit?"

"Sure, there's lots of room," said Nathan. "There's room for Meg too."

Claire thought it was a great idea. She worked to overcome her mother's concerns, assuring her there was no way any of them could fall out in the middle of the night.

"Hooray!" they all cried together when at last she agreed.

They began to make plans immediately.

"We'll need sleeping bags and foam sleeping pads," said Claire.

"Why don't we just lay down some blankets? That will be good enough," said Ryan. "It will be easier than trying to fit sleeping pads in the treehouse." The others agreed.

"What about meals?" asked Nathan, who was always most concerned with food.

"We can bring the camp stove," said Claire.

"Why don't we just have hot dogs for dinner?" said Kendra. "We can cook them over a campfire. That will be easy."

"And we can roast marshmallows and have s'mores!" said Nathan.

"I'll make you a salad you can take with you," said Aunt Jennie. "You have to eat something healthy!"

Claire and Ryan made a list of things they would need and started gathering them from the basement. Since they were only planning to go for one night and didn't need a tent, the list didn't seem too long. But they kept thinking of extra items to bring and before they knew it, there was quite a big pile of gear.

Kendra and Nathan organized the food under Aunt Jennie's watchful eye. They packed oatmeal and dried fruit for breakfast. As well as hot dogs and buns, they packed ketchup and mustard, and chocolate, marshmallows, and graham crackers to make s'mores for dessert. As she had promised, Aunt Jennie made a salad and put it in a cooler bag to keep fresh. She also added some muffins as an extra snack and removed a second bag of marshmallows which Nathan had tried to slip in.

When they were done organizing, they put most of the items into their backpacks. The food went into a separate cooler. They planned to carry their sleeping bags under their arms as it wasn't too far to the treehouse. If they had forgotten anything, they could always come back and get it.

"What else do we need?" said Claire, surveying their supplies.

"Tyler!" said Kendra. "We should invite him along. After all, he helped us build the treehouse."

"Good idea!" said Claire. She called Tyler from the phone in the other room. When she returned, she announced that he was coming. "He'll meet us there a little later in the afternoon," she said.

They set off after lunch. Ryan and Nathan carried the cooler between them, while Claire and Kendra brought the sleeping bags and blankets. Although it wasn't very far, it seemed a long way toting all their food and gear in the hot afternoon sun. When they arrived, they dumped it with relief at the base of the treehouse.

"Let's go for a swim. I'm dying of heat," said Ryan. They ran down the beach and into the water. There were shrieks and howls as they plunged in. The ocean had been stirred up by the big storm and was much chillier than it had been only a few days earlier. But it was refreshing after the hot walk to the treehouse and they soon got used to it. While they were swimming Tyler paddled into view. He pulled his canoe up on the shore and ran in to join them, splashing as he went. Afterward, they sat on the beach to dry off.

"Have you seen the rope swing?" asked Tyler, pointing down the beach.

"No," said Nathan. "What swing?"

"I saw it as I was paddling here. It's down at the other end of the beach. There's a tree hanging over the water with a rope hanging from one of the branches." The others looked where he was pointing. They could see a large tree near the water's edge and could just make out a rope dangling from it.

"That must be new. Let's go check it out!" said Nathan. He stood up and started running down the beach. The others followed behind.

The rope hung from a sturdy branch extending over the water. It was very thick with large knots tied in it every few feet.

"Is the water deep enough?" asked Ryan.

Tyler waded out until he could no longer touch the bottom. He swam to where the rope hung down and tried to dive down to the sea floor.

"It's pretty deep," he spluttered as he came up. "I can't touch the bottom."

Nathan was already pulling the rope back. He waited until Tyler was out of the way and then he jumped onto the rope and pushed off. He swung out over the water in a big arc, letting go at its highest point. He dropped into the water with a yell and a big splash.

"It's perfect!" he shouted, shaking the water from his head. "Go for it!"

The others needed no further encouragement, scrambling up the rocks to take their turn. They whooped and hollered as they swung through the air, each trying to outdo the other with how high they could swing, how far they could jump, or how big a splash they could make. Ryan landed with a big belly flop, which gained him the award for the biggest splash but left him gasping and spluttering as he swam to shore.

Tyler managed to twist himself around as he let go of the rope and did a perfect swan dive into the water. Everybody clapped and cheered. He didn't come up for a long time and when he did he was holding a shell in his hand.

"I managed to swim down and touch the bottom," he said, gasping for air. "But I couldn't see much, it's pretty deep."

They continued to play on the rope swing for the rest of the afternoon until the sun began to drop

Nathan swung out over the water in a big arc.

lower in the sky. Finally, they made their way back to the treehouse.

"I'm starving," said Nathan. "When's dinner?"

"When you've collected some firewood," said Claire.

"I'll help," said Kendra.

Together, Nathan and Kendra scoured the beach for driftwood. Soon they had a pile of small pieces to make a fire. They arranged a few large stones in a circle on the beach, well away from the trees. Filling the circle with twigs and dry grass, they lit it with a match. A thin trail of smoke emerged from the twigs, followed by small flames. They gingerly placed a few bits of wood on top and soon had a nice fire crackling away.

"Now we need roasting sticks," said Kendra. She went back to the top of the beach and found several sticks amongst the driftwood. Using Nathan's knife she carefully trimmed the ends of each one into a sharp point.

Claire brought over the cooler and pulled out the hot dogs and buns. Kendra handed everyone a roasting stick and they each placed a hot dog on it. Then they held them over the fire to cook. A delicious smell of roasting hot dogs wafted over them as they sizzled on the end of the sticks. When they were done, they placed them in the buns, slathered them in ketchup and mustard, and sat down on the beach to enjoy their dinner.

"Mmm, there's nothing better than a campfire meal," said Nathan. Everyone nodded in agreement. They all felt very contented sitting on the beach. It was a beautiful evening. The sea was calm and there was only the sound of the small fire crackling beside them. Just offshore a seal poked its head through the water and stared at them.

"I think it wants to come and share our food!" laughed Kendra.

When they finished their hot dogs, they each cooked another over the fire, and then a third. Nathan made to reach for a fourth, but Claire stopped him.

"Three's enough," she said. "Or you'll be too stuffed for marshmallows." Nathan was about to argue, but at the word 'marshmallows' he stopped and looked around for the bag.

"Hold on," she said, keeping the bag away from him. "We should get our sleeping bags set up first, so we don't have to do it in the dark."

"Good idea," said Ryan.

They went back to the treehouse and pulled their gear up with the rope and pulley. They spread the blankets on the floor and laid out their sleeping bags, leaving a spot for Meg in the corner.

"Don't forget the cooler," said Ryan. "We don't want any animals visiting in the middle of the night!"

Once everything was in the treehouse, it was completely full. The cooler was tucked behind the hatch and their backpacks and spare clothes were hung up on nails on the walls. Even so, there was no room to spare. Four sleeping bags were spread out side by side, with a fifth laid in the opposite direction at their feet. A nice space in the corner had been kept clear for Meg, but at the moment she was stretched out in the middle of the sleeping bags, leaving very little room for anyone else.

"You're going to have to move, Meg, before we go to sleep," said Kendra, wagging her finger at her. Meg just yawned and stretched, taking up even more space.

They climbed down the ladder and went back to the beach to roast marshmallows. They pushed the marshmallows onto the end of their roasting sticks and held them over the fire. It took great skill to get each one a perfect golden brown without getting too close to the flames or having it drop into the fire.

"Perfect," said Nathan, holding his marshmallow up for everyone to inspect. He pulled it off the stick and pressed it between the graham crackers and chocolate to make a s'more. "Mmm," he said, licking chocolate from his fingers.

Kendra wasn't so lucky. Her first one fell off into the fire and her second burst into flames just when she thought it was done. Finally, on her third attempt she had a perfect golden marshmallow, ready to be eaten.

"Hey look!" said Ryan, just as she was about to pop it in her mouth. "What are they doing here?"

The others followed his gaze out across the bay. Coming around the point was the big yacht from the harbour, pushing a foamy wake from its bow. The little submersible glowed in the evening sun, looking like a giant dragonfly on the back deck. The yacht slowed down and gently motored to the middle of the bay before stopping. The engines shifted into reverse and there was the sound of the anchor chain being let go.

"It looks like they're stopping for the night," said Tyler.

"It's not a very good place to anchor," said Claire, frowning. "If there's a storm they'll be completely exposed."

"The weather looks pretty good right now," said Ryan. There was no wind at all and the water was glassy calm.

"I suppose so," said Claire. "Or maybe they're not planning to stay too long."

Once the yacht was anchored, the engines turned off and it floated silently in the bay. They watched it for a bit longer and then turned their attention back to roasting marshmallows.

After his sixth s'more, Claire refused to let Nathan eat any more. He sat on the beach and licked the last bits of chocolate and marshmallow from his fingers. Glancing out at the yacht, he could see people moving about inside the cabin. Claire had brought a pair of binoculars, and Nathan went to fetch them from the treehouse in order to take a closer look.

Bringing the binoculars to his eyes, he focused on the yacht. As he did so, the cabin door opened and someone came out. Nathan trained the binoculars on him. It looked like the same man with short blond hair and long sideburns who had spoken to them in the harbour.

"Hey, there's the guy we saw in Maple Harbour," Nathan said. The others didn't pay him much attention as they were busy watching Tyler try to blow out a marshmallow that had caught on fire.

The man walked to the edge of the boat and stood with his hands on the railing. Nathan looked at him closely through the binoculars. He was wearing the same navy blue polo shirt and white shorts as before. It must be the ship's uniform, he thought. He lowered his gaze to the man's feet, which he could see through the railing.

Those are funny looking shoes, he thought. Black sneakers covered in polka dots.

Nathan thought for a moment. The shoes seemed vaguely familiar. Leaning forward, he adjusted the focus on the binoculars.

Suddenly, he froze.

Those weren't polka dots. They were paint splatters!

~14~

A Bold Plan

Nathan lowered the binoculars and stared out at the yacht. Then he turned to the others.

"Those are the shoes!" he said. "The ones I saw at the museum!"

"What are you talking about?" said Ryan.

Nathan realized he had never told them about the sneakers he'd seen protruding from the ceiling the day of the museum opening. The others had no idea what he was talking about. He explained quickly how he had gone looking for the washroom and stumbled into the wrong room, where he'd seen those shoes coming down from the ceiling before he'd escaped through the door and hurried away.

"And that guy on the yacht is wearing the same shoes as the person you saw at the museum?" asked Claire.

"So what?" said Ryan. "Black sneakers are pretty common. In fact, Tyler's wearing a pair right now." They all looked at Tyler, who stuck his foot out to show them his sneakers.

"Don't you see? It's not the sneakers, it's the paint splatters!" said Nathan. "There are lots of black sneakers, but not very many have paint splatters like that. It's got to be the same pair of shoes!"

"And if it's the same pair of shoes," said Tyler slowly. "Then that guy on the boat must have been up in the ceiling of the museum."

"Exactly!" said Nathan triumphantly, pleased that someone understood what he was getting at.

"But what would he be doing in the ceiling of the museum?" asked Kendra, still unclear as to why this seemed important to Nathan.

"I'm not sure. But maybe it has something to do with the break-in."

"Sergeant Sandhu said the alarm was disabled at some point," said Ryan. "Do you think he could have had something to do with that?"

"Wouldn't you have to be some sort of security expert to disable the alarm system?" said Tyler. "Not a marine biologist."

"You know, that's a funny thing," said Ryan. "Do you remember when he told us they were looking for starfish?" They nodded.

"I know lots of people call them starfish. But their real name is a sea star. You'd think a marine biologist would call them by their proper name."

"So if he's not a marine biologist, maybe he's not really a sailor either. Perhaps he's just pretending to be one so he could steal the mask," said Nathan excitedly.

"But how would he get in and know where to go?" said Kendra. "Someone would have had to let him in."

Now it was Claire's turn to look both excited and dismayed. "Jim Jenson," she said, her eyes wide. "The museum curator. I saw him coming off the yacht yesterday."

"Do you think he's in on it?" said Kendra.

"It's hard to believe," said Claire. "But why else would he be on board the yacht?"

"It all seems a bit far-fetched," said Tyler. "Besides, the guy on the yacht couldn't have been at the museum. The opening ceremony was last week, but the yacht only arrived in Maple Harbour two days ago."

"No it didn't!" Claire, Ryan, Kendra, and Nathan all cried out together. Tyler stared at them.

"They were somewhere nearby the day of the museum ceremony," said Claire, laughing at the confused expression on Tyler's face. She told him how they had seen the little submersible pass underneath them while they were out sailing. The very afternoon after the ceremony!

The whole thing was beginning to sound more plausible. But Ryan wasn't convinced.

"It's all just guesswork," he said. "We don't have any proof. Or even any real evidence."

"So let's get some," said Nathan.

"How?"

"Maybe we could sneak out to the yacht and look for evidence," said Tyler. They paused to think about this.

"Is that a good idea?" said Ryan. "What if we get caught?"

"We could just poke around a bit, maybe look in the portholes," said Claire. "We'll be careful."

Together they made a plan. They would wait until after dark and then paddle out to the yacht in Tyler's canoe. Maybe they would see something through the portholes that might confirm their suspicions.

Once the plan was set they tried to do other things to keep themselves busy. They roasted and ate all the remaining marshmallows. Then they played Frisbee on the beach for a while. But nothing could distract them from the task ahead. In the end, they sat on the beach by the fire, watching the yacht until the sun went down.

* * *

When it was completely dark they picked up Tyler's canoe and carried it to the water's edge, being careful not to make any noise. The sky had clouded over, hiding the moon, and the outline of the yacht was barely visible across the water.

There was only room for three in the canoe, so it was decided that Kendra and Nathan would stay with Meg. Although Nathan complained bitterly about being left behind, he was secretly glad to be safe on shore with Meg. They waved silently as the canoe set off, then sat down on the beach to wait.

Claire and Ryan paddled gently while Tyler sat in the middle of the canoe. Slowly they crossed the bay until they reached the yacht, pulling up alongside it.

"Let's see if we can look through those portholes," Claire said softly, pointing above their heads.

Tyler was the tallest of the three. He slowly stood up on the middle seat, placing his hands on the side of the yacht for support. Claire and Ryan tried to keep the canoe steady with their paddles, but it wobbled back and forth nonetheless.

Tyler stood on his tippy toes and stretched his neck up as far as he could, but he still couldn't see through the porthole. He sat back down dejectedly.

"It's too high up," he said. "We'll have to sneak on board."

Ryan looked at him incredulously. "Sneak on board?" he said. "Are you serious?"

"Tyler's right," said Claire. "We need to get on the boat if we're going to look around."

Ryan felt his stomach sink, but he didn't say anything. They manoeuvred the canoe around to the stern of the yacht. There was a transom at the back, a small deck low to the water onto which they could step quite easily. From there, a short ladder led up to the back deck of the yacht.

Claire and Tyler stepped quietly onto the transom. Ryan stayed in the canoe, hanging on to keep it from floating away. Claire slowly began to climb up the ladder. When she got to the top, she poked her head over and glanced around. Looking back, she gave a thumbs-up sign and climbed onto the deck. Tyler followed behind.

They found themselves behind the little submersible. Making their way around it, they stayed in the shadows to keep out of sight. Reaching the front of the submersible, they paused. Reassuring themselves that there was nobody about, they crossed the deck and crept along the side of the cabin until they came to a window.

Claire stood up and peeked in. A light was on but there was nobody in the room. It was a small cabin with a bed and a desk. There were a few books on the desk and some dirty clothes on the bed but not much else. She looked for signs of the mask or any other type of evidence, but there was nothing. Ducking down, she continued to move forward with Tyler following behind.

They went from window to window checking inside each cabin. Some rooms were dark or had the curtains closed so they couldn't see anything. The others showed no signs of the mask or any other clues. Reaching the front, they scurried across to the other side and made their way towards the stern, continuing their inspection of each cabin. Still they found nothing.

"What should we do now?" whispered Claire.

Tyler looked up. Above them they could see the upper deck. At the front was the bridge, with large windows and lots of light. Along the sides were more cabins. All were dark except one.

Tyler pointed up with a questioning look. Claire nodded her head. They'd come this far; they might as well continue.

They slowly climbed the steps to the upper deck. Silently making their way to the bow, they peeked into the bridge, staying in the shadows so as not to be seen. Inside, two crew members were leaning over a chart. But there was no sign of the mask. Claire sighed softly. Now there was only one more room to look at, on the far side.

The last room was a large cabin with a door to the outside deck. It was much bigger than the other cabins and quite luxurious. There were old charts on the walls and shelves with scale models of old sailing ships. This must be the owner's quarters, Claire thought.

The curtains were drawn, but Claire and Tyler could see part of the room through a gap in the curtains. At one end was an antique desk made of dark, rich wood. A cardboard box and some old books lay on top of it. Nothing they could see provided any clues to the missing mask.

"Nothing," said Claire, discouraged.

Tyler took another look through the window. Suddenly he tugged on Claire's sleeve and pointed.

"Look at the label on that box!" he whispered excitedly.

Claire stared at the label, trying to read it. It was difficult to see from that distance, but she could just make out the words: *Deliver to Maple Harbour Museum*.

"That box came from the museum!" she said.

"I know! And why would a box from the museum be here?"

"I wish we could see inside it," said Claire.

"Maybe we can," said Tyler. He reached for the door handle, but Claire pulled him back.

"We can't just go in," she said. "It's bad enough we're sneaking around on their boat, let alone breaking into a cabin."

"But what if the mask is in there?"

Suddenly, they heard a door open and a beam of light was cast onto the deck. Someone was coming from the bridge!

~15~

Pursuit

Claire and Tyler looked at each other in panic. Claire darted toward the stairs with Tyler right behind her. Moving as quickly as they could without making any noise, they scurried down the steps and looked for somewhere to hide. Spying the submersible, Claire threw herself underneath it into a small space between the ballast tanks and the hull. She squeezed over as Tyler followed her. They lay absolutely still, holding their breath.

On the upper deck they heard voices and then footsteps coming down the stairs. Peering out from under the submersible's hull, Claire spied two sets of feet at the bottom of the steps. Neither belonged to the man with the paint-splattered shoes.

"We'll leave in ten minutes," said a gruff, authoritative voice.

"Why so soon?" came the other voice. "What about our research?"

"It's what the boss wants," said the first voice. "We're heading back across the border."

The men moved on and disappeared from Claire's view. A door on the lower deck opened and the men went inside. Claire turned to Tyler.

"They're leaving," she whispered. "We've got to get off the boat!"

"We've got to get the mask!" answered Tyler. Before Claire could stop him, he wriggled out from under the submersible and ran across the deck!

From her viewpoint under the hull, Claire saw Tyler's feet vanish up the stairs. She slithered out from her hiding spot and just caught a glimpse of him as he went around the corner on the upper deck. She held her breath and waited.

Suddenly there was a yell, followed by a door slamming. Tyler came tearing back around the corner toward the stairs. Claire didn't wait to see what was happening. She dashed to the ladder that led to the back transom and scurried down it. Jumping into the front of the canoe, she picked up the paddle, ready to go.

"What's going on?" whispered Ryan.

Claire didn't answer. She watched as Tyler appeared at the top of the ladder. In his arms was the cardboard box. He climbed down the first few steps and then jumped the rest of the way onto the transom. Above they could hear angry voices shouting.

"I've got it!" said Tyler as he jumped into the canoe. "Let's go!"

Claire and Ryan needed no further encouragement. Already someone was on the deck with a large flashlight, pointing it in their direction. The beam lit up the canoe.

"There they are!" someone yelled. "It's a bunch of kids. They're in a canoe!"

Claire and Ryan paddled for all they were worth. This time Ryan didn't notice his arms getting sore at all. He was too focused on getting back to shore. In spite of the cool night air, he could feel beads of sweat gathering on his forehead.

Tyler sat in the middle clutching the cardboard box, his heart pounding. When he had opened the door to the cabin, the first thing he'd seen was someone dozing in a chair on the other side of the room. It was the owner of the yacht. Luckily, the box was close to the door, so he'd carefully lifted the lid and peeked inside. There was the missing mask! As he picked up the box, one of the old books on the desk had fallen to the floor with a bang. Tyler darted out of the room as the drowsy owner struggled to get out of his chair. He had just made it back to the canoe before the whole ship had been alerted.

Claire looked up from her paddling and could see Kendra, Nathan, and Meg standing on the shore. The clouds had parted and the beach was lit clearly by the moonlight. That means the people on the boat can see us too, thought Claire. She stopped paddling and caught her breath for a moment so she could call to the shore.

"We've got the mask!" she yelled. "Go get help!"

There was no movement from Kendra and Nathan, who stood frozen where they were. Only Meg showed that she'd heard, trotting toward them and wagging her tail. She barked excitedly.

"Call the police!" Claire yelled again. This time they must have heard because suddenly both of them turned and ran toward the trail that led to the house. Meg hesitated a moment, looking back and forth, unsure whether to follow or wait for Claire. Then she dashed after Kendra and Nathan.

There was the sound of a motor starting and Tyler turned back to look at the yacht.

"Hurry, they're launching the inflatable dinghy!" he said.

"We're going as fast as we can!" said Ryan between laboured breaths.

The canoe was about three-quarters of the way to shore, but Claire knew the dinghy would catch up quickly. At the end of the beach, she spied Kendra and Nathan disappearing into the forest trail.

Paddling with every ounce of strength they had, the canoe finally landed on the beach. Claire hopped out and began to pull the canoe up out of the water.

"Never mind the canoe," said Tyler. "Just run!"

The three started running toward the forest trail. But the dinghy steered to the right to cut them off. Before they could reach the trail, the dinghy landed on the shore and two burly men jumped out. One of them was the blond-haired man with the long sideburns. He was no longer smiling.

"Go back!" cried Claire. She stopped in her tracks and turned the other way, only to collide with Tyler, knocking them both to the ground. He dropped the cardboard box and the mask flew out, tumbling down the beach before coming to a stop at the water's edge.

"Grab the mask!" yelled Tyler. Ryan ran over and picked it up.

"Ryan, take the mask and hide!" said Claire. "We'll distract them!"

The two men were closing in on them quickly. Picking themselves up, Claire and Tyler ran toward the opposite end of the beach, while Ryan cut diagonally toward the forest.

Suddenly the moon passed behind a cloud, throwing everything momentarily into darkness. Ryan seized the opportunity to veer off into the trees. He clambered over the driftwood logs piled at the top of the beach, clutching the mask with one hand and balancing himself with the other. Ducking into the forest, he turned to look back. His plan seemed to have worked. The two men hadn't seen him enter the woods and were running along the beach after Claire and Tyler.

Ryan doubled back and began to make his way through the forest in the direction of the trail. It was very dark in the trees and he had trouble seeing where he was going. There were cries in the distance and he worried that the men had caught up to Claire and Tyler. If so, they would soon realize that they didn't have the mask.

He was making such slow progress in the trees that he decided to return to the beach. Emerging from the forest, he ran swiftly alongside the piles of driftwood. The moon was out again, lighting up the bay.

Suddenly, there was a shout and he knew he'd been spotted. Sure enough, the two men were only a short distance away and heading in his direction. In a panic, he turned back into the trees. He took a few steps and then tripped over a root, falling to his knees. Looking up he saw a wooden step nailed into the tree in front of him. He was at the treehouse.

Without thinking, Ryan grasped hold of the step and pulled himself up. He raced up the wooden ladder and pushed open the hatch. Throwing the mask onto the sleeping bags in front of him, he pulled himself into the treehouse and crawled into the corner. He rolled over and sat with his back against the wall, his heart pounding.

As he sat there, it dawned on him that maybe the treehouse wasn't the best place to hide. There was no escaping if they found him. He would just have to hope they didn't.

The minutes passed slowly with no sound from the men. Ryan began to feel hopeful they had moved further down the beach. But then he heard one of them curse as they slipped on a piece of driftwood. They were getting closer!

Moments later Ryan heard a twig snap directly below the treehouse. He suddenly realized he had forgotten to close the hatch after he crawled in. Now the beam of a flashlight shone through the opening, illuminating the roof above him. He held his breath, his heart beating wildly.

The wooden steps creaked. The two men were climbing up to the treehouse!

~16~

Meg's Surprise

Ryan's mind raced. He didn't know what to do. Should he try to close the hatch? But it was too late—they were almost at the top.

Clutching the mask in front of him, he crouched in the corner of the treehouse. He could just make out the mask's features in the moonlight. The large eyes stared out at him and the sharp white teeth gleamed. He remembered Kendra saying how scary it looked, even in the light of the museum. Now, in the dark, it looked truly ferocious.

A pair of hands appeared at the edge of the hatch and Ryan's heart skipped a beat. Suddenly he had an idea. Placing the mask to his face, he turned towards the hatch. Then, with a ferocious roar, he leaped toward the opening just as the blond man's head appeared!

The man's eyes grew wide with terror, and he threw up his hands to protect himself. Ryan landed on the man's shoulders, forcing him back against the hatch opening. The next thing he knew the man was falling away from him, down the tree. There was a

With a ferocious roar he leaped towards the opening.

cry followed by a loud grunt as he landed on the second man, who was climbing the ladder below. Then there was a heavy thud as both of them hit the ground.

"My leg, my leg!" shrieked one of the men in agony.

Ryan had to stop himself from falling through the opening after them. He grasped the edge of the hatch and peered down. The two men were lying on the ground, not moving. The second man was holding his leg and moaning while the blond man seemed to be unconscious.

Ryan didn't waste any time. Holding the mask, he scrambled down the ladder. Halfway down he stopped and jumped, landing a safe distance from the two men. The one with the injured leg didn't notice him but the blond man was stirring and looked at him groggily as he landed. He started to get to his feet as Ryan took off through the forest toward the beach.

Ryan burst out of the trees and clambered over the driftwood onto the beach. He tried to balance himself with one hand as he held onto the mask with the other. Behind him, he could hear the man breathing heavily.

Reaching the beach, Ryan took off as fast as he could. He ran in the direction of the trail, where he could see a light coming in the distance.

"Over here!" he yelled. "Help! Help!"

As he called out, he felt a hand grab onto his shoulder and suddenly he was thrown down on the beach. He landed hard on his stomach and felt the wind knocked out of him. The mask flew out of his hand.

"Thank you very much!" the man growled as he picked up the mask. He turned and strode toward the dinghy.

Ryan managed to get up on his hands and knees. Then he felt something wet against his cheek.

"Meg!" he said, giving her a hug as she licked his face. Up ran Kendra and Nathan followed by Uncle William. They were all asking him questions at once.

"What happened?"

"Are you all right?"

"Where's Claire? Where's Tyler?"

"Where's the mask?"

Ryan just shook his head and pointed down the beach, where the man was pushing the dinghy into the water. "He's getting away!" he gasped.

Uncle William took off down the beach toward the dinghy with Meg hot on his heels. The outboard

motor started with a roar and the dinghy shot off.
Meg rushed after it, jumping through the waves and
barking loudly. Uncle William stopped running and
watched as the dinghy sped off toward the yacht.

They all watched in dismay as the dinghy disappeared into the darkness. Ryan felt a terrible sinking
feeling in his stomach. The thieves were getting away
and their efforts had been for nothing. All because he
tried to hide in the treehouse instead of in the forest,
he thought bitterly.

Suddenly there was an awful tearing sound, followed by a cry and a loud splash. Moments later the
dinghy engine went silent.

"What happened?" said Nathan.

"It sounds like he hit something," said Kendra.
They peered into the darkness, trying to see.

"That old piece of machinery!" said Ryan. "I
think he hit it! Wasn't it around that spot?"

"You're right!" said Nathan. "That's exactly
where it was."

"And the tide is quite low, so it would have been
sticking out of the water," added Kendra.

Their faces turned to wide grins as they realized
what had occurred. Uncle William rejoined them and
they told him what they thought had happened. He
laughed along with them.

"Well, he certainly got what he deserved," he said. "Although I hope he can swim," he continued, looking a bit concerned.

Behind them they heard more voices coming down the trail. A bright flashlight shone toward them. It was Aunt Jennie with Sergeant Sandhu and another police officer. They ran up to them.

Ryan explained to Sergeant Sandhu what had happened. Nathan led the other officer to the tree-house, where the second man from the yacht was still lying on the ground moaning. She handcuffed him before calling for an ambulance. It seemed that he had broken his leg when he fell from the tree.

Sergeant Sandhu swept his powerful flashlight over the water where they had last seen the dinghy. At length, they saw a figure wading ashore, his clothes dripping wet. Sergeant Sandhu marched down the beach to meet him, where the blond man gave himself up, too exhausted to protest.

Out in the bay, the engines on the yacht suddenly came to life and they heard the anchor chain being raised. The yacht turned around and set off to the south at full speed.

"Oh no, they're getting away!" said Kendra.

Sergeant Sandhu smiled. "Not to worry," he said. "They won't get far. The police boat is already on its way." He pulled out a radio and spoke into it briefly, passing on the information. Sure enough, another boat soon came into view. A huge spotlight lit up the yacht and a bullhorn echoed across the water, ordering it to stop. The yacht kept going, but the police boat soon intercepted them.

"Is that everyone?" Sergeant Sandhu asked Ryan. Sergeant Sandhu looked past him down the beach. "Wait a minute. Who's that?"

Two figures were running down the beach. It was Claire and Tyler. They arrived out of breath. Everyone started talking at once, asking each other questions without waiting to hear the answer.

"Wait a minute," said Tyler. "Where's the mask?"

Everyone stopped talking. In all the excitement, they had forgotten about the mask.

"It was in the dinghy," said Ryan, looking over at the man standing handcuffed next to Sergeant Sandhu.

"He didn't have it with him when he came ashore," said Sergeant Sandhu. "So it must still be out there."

They all gazed out to sea. If the mask was floating out there, the winds and currents could carry it anywhere. Sergeant Sandhu shone his flashlight over the water, but they couldn't see anything. Only Meg, happily trotting along the beach.

"Come here Meg!" called Nathan. She ran up and he bent down to pet her. "What's that you've got?"

Meg proudly dropped something at his feet. He picked it up and began to laugh. He held it up triumphantly for everyone to see.

"Here it is!" he said. "Meg found the mask!"

~17~

More Rhubarb

A few days later they were all gathered on the back deck for dinner. Tyler had joined them, as well as Sergeant Sandhu. Uncle William had caught a large salmon that morning and grilled it on the barbecue. Now Aunt Jennie was serving it with roasted potatoes and a big salad full of fresh vegetables from the garden.

"Mmm," said Kendra, taking a bite of salmon. "I haven't had salmon since, well, this time last year."

Aunt Jennie laughed. "There's lots, so eat as much as you like." She turned to Sergeant Sandhu. "Raj, have some more potatoes."

"Don't mind if I do," he said. "It's hard work fighting crime all day!"

Claire looked at him and rolled her eyes. Maple Harbour was pretty sleepy—most of the time!

"Speaking of crime, did you catch the museum curator?" asked Ryan.

"Yes, we caught him yesterday," replied Sergeant Sandhu. "We got a tip that he might be in a cabin up the coast, and when we went to check it out, he was hiding there."

"So how was Jim Jenson involved, anyway?" asked Uncle William. "I never quite understood that part."

"It seems he had serious money problems," said Sergeant Sandhu. "He'd made several bad investments and ended up in serious debt. He borrowed a lot of money from Robert Borman, who he knew through his connections in the world of maritime antiquities. But when he couldn't pay it back, Borman forced him to steal the mask.

"Borman was a fanatical collector. He wanted to have the best collection of maritime antiquities in the world. When he heard about the mask he became obsessed with getting hold of it. Having the museum curator in debt to him played right into his hands."

"So what did the blond man with the paint-splattered shoes have to do with it?" asked Kendra.

"His name is Gerald Larsen. He's a career criminal with a long list of convictions. He's an expert at disabling security systems."

"I knew it!" said Ryan. "He couldn't be a marine biologist!"

"That's right," said Sergeant Sandhu. "The rest of the crew were as confused as you were. Larsen didn't know much about marine biology or boats, so they couldn't understand why Borman had hired him for this trip. Most of the crew had no idea what was going on. Only a couple of them were involved."

"So Borman hired Larsen, and Jim Jenson let him into that electrical room where Nathan saw him during the opening ceremony?" said Tyler.

"Right. The curator couldn't just disarm the alarm system and take the mask. He was the only one who knew the alarm codes, so everyone would know who had done it. But it was actually the curator who came back and took the mask later that night, once the system was disabled."

"Why didn't they just take the mask and leave right away?" asked Tyler.

"We couldn't understand that at first, either," said Sergeant Sandhu. "If they'd collected the mask and left right away, they might never have been caught. It turns out that Jim Jenson was asking for more money. He realized the mask was worth a lot more than what he owed Borman, so he refused to give it up until he got some extra cash."

"So being greedy caused them to all get caught," said Kendra.

"It did indeed."

They finished their dinner and Claire and Ryan cleared the dishes before Aunt Jennie brought out dessert.

"What, no rhubarb pie tonight?" asked Nathan.

"No, something different." She placed a glass dish down on the table. "Rhubarb crumble!"

Claire and Nathan pretended to groan. But there was no complaining once they had a bowl of crumble in front of them. The tangy rhubarb was a perfect complement to the sweet brown sugar and oats, topped off with creamy vanilla ice cream.

"So what will happen to the mask?" asked Ryan, once they had stuffed themselves with second helpings of crumble.

"We're still holding it as evidence," replied Sergeant Sandhu. "But we should be able to return it to the museum in a few days."

"Is the mask okay?" asked Claire. "I hope Meg didn't do any damage to it." Upon hearing her name, Meg looked up from her place beside the table. She was patiently waiting to see if any leftover salmon would find its way into her dinner bowl!

"No, it seems to be fine after all its adventures. We had an expert come in from the city to look it over. He said that no damage had been done, either by Meg or by being dunked in the ocean.

"It's a good thing Meg found it. It could have drifted out to sea. If that had happened, it might have been days or weeks before we found it."

"Or not at all," said Tyler. "It's pretty hard to find something that small floating around in the ocean."

"You saved the day, Meg!" said Nathan, putting his arms around her as she licked his face. "Maybe they'll put up a statue of her in front of the museum!"

"Or maybe I should keep her as a special police dog," said Sergeant Sandhu with a grin.

"No way!" said Kendra. "We need her here to help us solve the next Maple Harbour mystery!"

Whatever that might be!

The End

About the Author

Michael Wilson lives in Gibsons, British Columbia with his family and dog, Meg. When not writing, he likes to sail his Flying Junior in the waters of Howe Sound. The Mystery of the Missing Mask is his second book for children.

* * *

Did you enjoy reading *The Mystery of the Missing Mask?* We'd love to hear from you!

Rainy Bay Press
PO Box 1911
Gibsons, BC
V0N 1V0

www.rainybaypress.ca

Look for more adventures with Claire, Ryan, Kendra, Nathan, and Meg, coming soon!

Don't miss the first Maple Harbour Adventure!

Adventure on Whalebone Island

Ryan and Kendra have come to Maple Harbour on the BC coast to spend their summer holidays with their aunt and uncle. They're expecting a leisurely holiday swimming and playing on the beach with their cousins Claire and Nathan. Claire, however, has other ideas— exploring islands in her sailboat and searching for sunken treasure. But what's hidden on mysterious Whalebone Island? Have the four of them come across a secret that others don't want discovered?

Join Ryan, Kendra, Claire, Nathan, and their dog Meg as they try to solve the mystery of a missing boat. What awaits the children is an even bigger, more dangerous mystery! I couldn't put this book down!

Colleen H., Teacher

Adventure on Whalebone Island reminded me of falling in love with reading classic adventure stories as a child. Maria M., parent

I loved the book! It had mystery, and I'd love to be on an adventure just like these kids in the story. Ava, age 10

Shortlisted for the 2017
BC Reader's Choice Children's Book Award
(Chocolate Lily Award)